"Andrea? It's Josh Walker."

She'd just been wishing to hear his voice, just been wishing for the comfort of his presence.

"Josh. How are you?" She shook the envelope and let the contents slide into her hand.

Whatever Josh's answer was, it was drowned out by the sudden buzz in her ears. Staring up at her from the photo in her hand was her own face as she spoke to the homeless man who often dropped by the office. Red ink scrawled across the image. *Stop what you're doing.* The image was taken through the scope of a rifle, crosshairs centered on her forehead.

In Josh's mind flashed giant red lights. "What's going on? Talk to me, Andrea."

The silence stretched on too long. "Someone sent me pictures." Andrea's voice held a measured control that did nothing to ease his mind. "Of me. At the counseling center. Two days ago."

Josh would not let this happen. He'd failed to act the last time. This time would be different. "I'm coming over. Call the police."

Books by Jodie Bailey

Love Inspired Suspense

Freefall
Crossfire

JODIE BAILEY

has been weaving stories since she learned how to hold a pencil. It was only recently she learned that everyone doesn't make up whole other lives for fun in their spare time. She is an army wife, a mom and a teacher who believes chocolate and a trip to the Outer Banks will cure all ills. In her spare time, she reads cookbooks, rides motorcycles and searches for the perfect cup of coffee. Jodie lives in North Carolina with her husband and her daughter.

Crossfire

Jodie Bailey

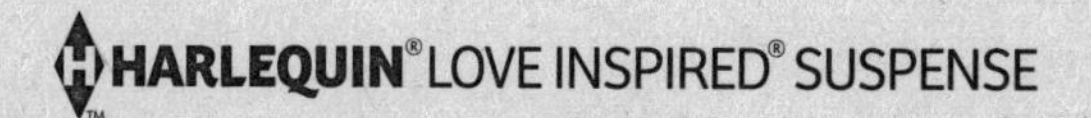

If you purchased this book without a cover you should be aware that this book is stolen property. It was reported as "unsold and destroyed" to the publisher, and neither the author nor the publisher has received any payment for this "stripped book."

Recycling programs for this product may not exist in your area.

ISBN-13: 978-0-373-44581-3

CROSSFIRE

Copyright © 2014 by Jodie Bailey

All rights reserved. Except for use in any review, the reproduction or utilization of this work in whole or in part in any form by any electronic, mechanical or other means, now known or hereafter invented, including xerography, photocopying and recording, or in any information storage or retrieval system, is forbidden without the written permission of the editorial office, Love Inspired Books, 233 Broadway, New York, NY 10279 U.S.A.

This is a work of fiction. Names, characters, places and incidents are either the product of the author's imagination or are used fictitiously, and any resemblance to actual persons, living or dead, business establishments, events or locales is entirely coincidental.

This edition published by arrangement with Love Inspired Books.

® and TM are trademarks of Love Inspired Books, used under license. Trademarks indicated with ® are registered in the United States Patent and Trademark Office, the Canadian Trade Marks Office and in other countries.

www.Harlequin.com

Printed in U.S.A.

He heals the brokenhearted and binds up their wounds.
—*Psalms* 147:3

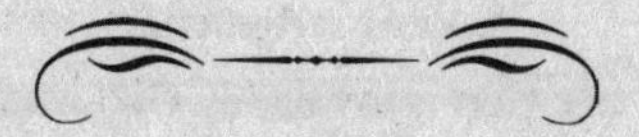

To Paul—God blessed me with you
beyond my wildest dreams. Everything I ever asked Him for?
You're so much more.

To Cailin—You are God's greatest gift to me and your daddy.
I love you to the moon and back, to infinity and beyond.

Acknowledgments

Dad, I believe God is my daddy God who loves me, because you showed me what sacrificial, unconditional love from a father really looks like. Thank you.

Mom, you are my biggest, loudest cheerleader. Thank you!

Emily Rodmell, you are the queen of editors. I love getting edits back from you and seeing how much better everything is after you've stepped alongside and poured into it. Thank you, thank you for taking these words and making them sing!

Kimberly Buckner, Donna Moore and Christina Nelson, you are prayer warriors, partners and friends of the deepest part of my heart. God definitely knew what He was doing when He threw a bunch of random strangers together. Lucky 13!

My "beta readers," Glenda Cook, Dawn Lucowitz, Jennifer McCarty and Kristin Dudish, thank you for the time and the attention to detail that made *Crossfire* what it is. I'm in awe....

Lesley Cooper, "my Lesley," who shouts across parking lots when I finish a book, who gives ear to my whining and loves me anyway. Laura Ott, this wouldn't have happened if you hadn't taken on my daughter as your own and if you hadn't let me just talk and talk. Laura Harris... you know what you did, Rock Star.

My church family, you are prayer warriors and awesome supporters, as are you, Freedom Christian family!

Paul and Cailin, you put up with deadlines, meltdowns, M&M binges and Mommy hunched over the computer for hours. I couldn't do this if you didn't cheer me on. Thank you, thank you, thank you.

Jesus. Oh, Jesus. You truly do make all things new.

ONE

Andrea Donovan stood at the glass-fronted entrance of her counseling center and watched the last patient of the day trek across the broiling parking lot to his car. The heat of the July Georgia sun blunted the edges of the world, giving the appearance that everything outside lay underwater. Her client eased onto Victory Drive, leaving her car alone in the parking lot save for a pickup truck idling near the gas station that neighbored her building.

Andrea looked out for a moment longer before she headed back to her office to shut down her computer and collect her files. She still had notes to make for her last patient, but all of her energy seemed to have drained into a pool at her feet. So many hurting people walked through her doors. It drained her, but in a way that made the end of the day seem more satisfying than brutal.

After gathering a stack of old documents for the shredder, Andrea stepped out to the empty reception desk in the lobby.

An unfamiliar man blocked her path. Adrenaline rocketed from Andrea's core and tingled in her fingertips.

Broad-shouldered, dark-haired and square-jawed, in jeans and a navy button-down shirt, he effectively blocked the small space between the desk and the door. His bulk and the determined expression chiseled on his face radiated menacing vibes that plucked at Andrea's flight response.

She took a step back, but the only place to run was to her windowless office. No outlet there. Swallowing hard, she drew herself up to her full five feet and six inches. It had better look more imposing than it felt. "Can I help you?"

The man's dark eyes raked over her, sizing her up and dismissing her as less threatening than a June bug. "You're Donovan? The counselor lady?" His posture said he wasn't here to ask for help.

"I am. Is there something I can do for you?" She gripped the papers tighter, wishing for the first time for the rifle she'd carried in combat on active duty six years ago. Not that she'd use it, but the knowledge that it was available would go miles toward making her feel safer in this guy's presence.

"I need to talk to you about Wade Cameron. You're his head doc, right?" His eyes took in the papers in Andrea's arms, then drifted over her head, scanning her office. "Where's he at?"

"He's certainly not here." Her mind flipped through her calendar. Army Specialist Wade Cameron hadn't been to see her in weeks. He'd graduated from weekly counseling sessions to AA meetings and conversations with his sponsor.

"Sure he's not." A cold half smile quirked the man's mouth in a way that was anything but comforting. "You won't mind if I take a look around then? Maybe get a peek at your file on him? Seems he might have left a message in there for me."

Andrea arched an eyebrow as her fear dissolved into fierce she-wolf protection. Specialist Cameron was one of her success stories, fighting his way out of a vicious cycle of PTSD-fueled alcohol addiction. The way he laughed so easily and carried himself with such dignity reminded her too much of Brendan, making her realize how much she had to make up for. No way was this street thug going to bully her into giving up confidential information on that kid.

She spaced her feet wider and squared her shoulders. If she got the man talking, maybe it would buy time to work her way around him to the door. "And you are?" From this angle, there was no view of the parking lot, but she desperately hoped someone driving by on Victory Drive would get a clue as to what was happening.

"You got a nice place here. Still smells a little like fresh paint sometimes, huh? You've been open here, what? Six months?" He stepped closer. "Shame if something should happen to this building if you don't stop what you're doing."

Andrea's knees weakened. She gripped the edge of the desk. "What's that supposed to mean? Who are you?" Only God could have gotten those words out of her mouth without them trembling.

"Just admiring your pretty building. And its…interesting location. Now…" He took one more step toward Andrea as she held her ground. "I am here to find my friend and to get a look at his file." The man's voice dropped as his jaw hardened. "If that's not asking too much of you. If it is, you can step out of the way and let me find it myself. Or I can move you. You can choose."

Without taking the time for her mind to process the action, Andrea reached behind her, jammed the lock, and yanked the office door shut as the man lunged. In less than a blink, his body thudded into the heavy wooden door as she sidestepped around him, adrenaline charging through her on electric rails.

She lunged for the front door and the relative safety of the parking lot. Just as her fingertips made contact with the glass, a corded arm snapped around her waist and jerked her back, lifting her feet from the floor.

"Very, very bad idea, Doc." The voice rumbled against her ear and washed cold fear down her spine. "I want the kid. And if you can't give me the kid, I want his file, because I need what's in it. And if you can't give me that, then you can come with me and tell me everything you know. As far as I'm concerned, that's the easiest way to solve two very big problems." He yanked her tighter against his chest. "Sound like a good plan to you?"

No. She struggled against the weight that held her back, clawed at the sleeves of his shirt, kicked at the air. Her mind searched her old army training for a way out. He held her too tight for an elbow to the ribs, too high for a heel to the instep. In a feat of sheer muscle memory, she jerked her head back as hard as she could and connected with the soft tissue of his nose.

Her attacker roared, and his grip loosened enough for her to break free and drop to the floor. Her knees and hands struggled for grip on the ancient tile.

His hands clamped around her ankle as her fingertips brushed the door and jerked her away from the only chance she had at freedom. Andrea scratched at the gray tile, clawing for traction, her fingernails catching a rough edge and ripping off. This would not be her end, on the floor of her own lobby. With a silent prayer and the last of her energy, she threw herself onto her back, her ankle twisting in her attacker's grip, and kicked her free foot straight up.

The sound of teeth crunching together echoed through

the room as her heel connected with the stranger's chin and drove his head back.

He staggered back, hands covering his face, teetering as though he might fall.

Andrea skittered across the floor and half rose in a backward drive for freedom.

With a howl that should have shaken the windows, the man ripped his hands from his face, blood slinging across the floor, and roared toward her again, his eyes glinting black murder.

As his fingers grasped her forearm and jerked her forward in a grip that felt like iron, the door opened and Andrea struggled for footing. As she did, a solid object crashed into the back of her shoulders, doubling her over as a second attacker rammed into her, knocking her onto her face.

There was a crash, a grunt and the sounds of fists on flesh. A swift kick jolted her thigh, as someone vaulted over her and out the door, then there was only silence, save the heavy breathing of the one man left in the lobby.

Andrea pushed to her hands and knees as fast as her shaking limbs would allow. Dragging in what might be her last breath, she steeled herself and prepared to go down fighting.

First Sergeant Josh Walker scrambled up, his first instinct to aid the woman on the floor, but he had to catch the man who had done this to her. He charged out the door in time to watch a burgundy sedan rocket out of the parking lot in a spray of dust and tire smoke. A groan roiled in the back of his throat as he balled his fists in frustration. The car was definitely a Chevy, but it was too far away to get the license plate. There was no way the police would arrive on the scene before that clown blended in with the end-of-duty-day traffic on Victory Drive.

The soft scrape of the door opening behind him pulled him to more immediate concerns. The woman. In the lobby. Nausea coiled in his stomach and looped through the familiar burn of condemnation. He'd chased off her attacker but had failed to catch him. He never seemed to quite follow through.

Josh pivoted and drew back as the woman's fist rocketed toward his head. He ducked to one side, but his awkward stance kept him from moving fast enough. The solid blow caught him square on his cheekbone, shooting stars through his field of vision. A series of rapid blinks cleared his eyesight in time to watch her rear back for round two.

Steadying himself on the door frame, he caught her fist with his free hand, squeezing a little tighter than he would have if she hadn't just coldcocked him. "Hey, hey. I'm the good guy. I promise." Leftover adrenaline edged his words and clouded his vision.

She jerked her arm to free herself from his grip, and he eased up a little, recognizing the fringes of hysteria in her green eyes. "Look at me." He dropped his voice to what he hoped was a soothing whisper, the one that used to work on his black lab during rocking thunderstorms. "Look at me. You're safe."

Her attention finally focused on him and, as the energy dissipated, he relaxed his hold on her hand only to tighten it again in a jolt of recognition. Andrea Donovan? The world couldn't possibly be that small.

The way her jaw slackened spoke more than words. It was her. And what was more amazing…she recognized him, too.

"Josh Walker?" His name rode an exhale barely above a whisper, one that held as much incredulity as he felt.

Josh nodded once, his voice free-falling to the pit of his stomach. It was ridiculous he hadn't recognized her sooner. It couldn't be possible that the last time he'd laid eyes on Andrea had been right out of high school. Too many years ago. He should do now what he'd been so tempted to do then, pull her close and shield her from the pain that tried to beat its way into her life.

With a deep sigh and a shake of her head, Andrea extricated herself from his grip and stepped back. She winced and stumbled as her weight shifted to her right foot.

Josh reached out and grasped the arms of the woman he had tried so often to forget, keeping her from slumping to the floor. Shoving his shock aside, he focused on the task at hand. Blending the past with the present was more than his brain could handle at this point. "Take it easy. You took a pretty vicious twist when you whipped around on him. Nice blow to the jaw, by the way." His lip curved into a wry smile. "His, not mine." When she didn't respond, his practiced eyes took in her pale face and tight lips. "You okay?"

Nodding, she let him open the door and lead her into the lobby where she sank down onto one of the brown pleather chairs in the small waiting room. "I'm fine."

Her shaking hands said differently, but Josh kept his mouth shut. He had no right to ask more of her. And given her current agitation, she might decide to swing again.

"Where did you come from?" she asked him.

Josh knelt in front of her but kept his distance. "The parking lot."

The look she fired his way let him know he'd completely misunderstood the question. "I meant how did you wind up here in my office?"

Yeah, it sent him reeling, too, seeing her out of context like this. He tapped his chest where his rank anchored to the front of his uniform. "First sergeant in Third Infantry. I joined the army during college." He swallowed hard against rising memories about why he signed up, and switched gears on the conversation. "Any idea who that guy was?"

Still clearly on high alert, Andrea shook her head and stared at the door. Was it the attack or him that caused her muscles to tense?

His eyes followed hers, but there was no movement outside in the summer heat. After a quick scan to make sure no one lurked behind the lone car still out there, Josh pushed himself to his feet and glanced at the desk behind him. More than anything, he needed distance. "I'm going to call the police so they can be on the lookout. I can identify the car. Can you give them a description of the guy?"

The tremors moved from her hands, up her arms and through her body. She wrapped her arms around her stomach and looked up at him. "Definitely. And after you call the police you can call a locksmith. I locked my car keys in my office and the only other set is at my apartment." Her lips twisted into a rueful, if shaky, smile. "And my apartment keys are on the same key ring. That just caps my day, doesn't it? First I get jumped, and now I can't go home."

Her green eyes latched on to his, as if she was looking for confirmation that it was okay to relax. They were the color of those old-fashioned Coke bottles, clearer and purer than he remembered. For a second, Josh couldn't break away, but he shook it off and forced himself to go make the call. She'd probably give him a black eye if she could read his thoughts. He'd seen her in action.

"So, Andrea." It had been so many years since he'd spoken her name that it felt foreign on his tongue. "This is your office? You started this place?" The chaplain had passed on the information about the counseling center to his chain of command, but he'd never heard her name associated with it.

"Yeah." She shuddered and flexed the fingers of the hand that had recently met his cheek. "I'm sorry I tried to deck you."

"No worries. Given the circumstances, it's understandable." Josh bit back a smile as he picked up the phone and took note of the stack of business cards on the counter. *Andrea Donovan.* So she wasn't married, unless she was one of those women who refused to take her husband's name. Not that he should be noticing.

The name still fit her as it always had, soft and girlish at first glance, but tough on the next look. The admiration building in him quenched itself under a heavy dose of guilt. She wouldn't have had to be tough if he'd have come to the rescue earlier. Then again, it looked as if she'd done a pretty good job of rescuing herself. Ten seconds more and she probably wouldn't have needed him at all.

Or she'd have been dead. He shook off the thought. There was no sense living in what might have been, especially when God had definitely kept the worst from happening. And there was no other explanation for this bizarre twist to his day, no other reason for him to be here other than to watch over her, to somehow fix what he'd broken years ago.

After a brief conversation with the police, Josh sank into a chair near Andrea. "You doing okay?"

She looked up from flexing her ankle. "I'm still here, thanks to you, and my ankle hurts less every second. All in all, it ended better than it should have." Before Josh could dig deeper, she rested her foot on the floor and gripped her knees. "What are you doing here, anyway?"

Josh sprang to his feet, his pulse quickening and driving hammers into the impact point on his cheek. He never should have forgotten why he was here in the first place. "Specialist Cameron. Where is he?"

The question barely ended before Andrea reacted. Eyes narrowed, nostrils flared, she stood gingerly and faced off, fists clenched. "What's going on, Josh?"

Prickles of fear crawled up Andrea's spine and spread into her fingernails. The boy she'd known years ago was now the man who happened into her office at just the right time? Two men bursting in to ask about the same young soldier? More than a dozen years had passed since she last laid eyes on Josh, and there was no way to tell what he'd gotten into in the intervening time. For all intents and purposes, he was as much a stranger as the giant she'd kicked in the face.

Andrea crossed her arms and squared her shoulders. Her mind whirled for a way to escape while her ankle protested enough to let her know in no uncertain terms that she couldn't expect to make a run for it and get very far. *Take control of the situation. Buck his authority. Let him know you're in charge.* "What do you want with Specialist Cameron?"

Perplexity floated across the brown eyes that locked on to hers. Josh's eyebrows drew together in a *V*, betraying his confusion at her barely concealed accusation. "He's one of my soldiers. Where is he?" His gaze darted around the room, taking in each corner.

"Clearly, he's not here. And your friend who just ran out of here got the same speech from me. I won't tell you the last time I saw Specialist Cameron, but I will tell you it wasn't today." Andrea held her breath and stiffened her spine, unwilling to believe Josh could be on the wrong side of this, but knowing she had to protect herself and Wade if he was.

"My friend?" He looked back to her, and a sudden flicker of understanding darkened his features. "Wait a second. You think I was with the punk who just busted in here and tried to tear you into pieces?"

"You're both asking for the same person. That's a little too much of a coincidence, don't you think?" Indignation surged through Andrea, and she fought to hold it back. Her ankle might be throbbing, but her fists were ready to fly. She'd show this dark-eyed man he'd messed with the wrong woman if he so much as breathed too hard. He'd have more than a bruised cheek to worry about if...

She tilted her head. Had she actually given him that bruise? Smug warmth heated her face. Sweet. She still had it, even at thirty-two and after six years of sitting behind a desk.

Josh cleared his throat. "I have no idea what your first visitor wanted, but I can tell you that at approximately 1630 I watched Specialist Wade Cameron walk through those doors—" he jerked his thumb behind him "—and take a left turn." His eyes scanned the lobby and lit on a door as his words evaporated into the muggy air.

Andrea tipped her head, still tensed for a fight. What was he talking about? "Wade never came in here. At 4:30 I was halfway through a fifty-minute session. With my receptionist Grace on vacation, Wade would have sat right here in these chairs and waited if you dropped him off here." She stepped between Josh and the door he still eyed. "That's a supply closet. The only other way out of this building is down that hall." She pointed behind her to an opening near her office, on the opposite side of the lobby from the closet. "But that door's always locked and it's armed with a fire alarm. The only way out without making a racket is to unlock it and turn it off with the key, and only my receptionist and I have one."

"He's in that closet, then. I never saw him come back across the lobby, and there's nowhere else in here he could be," Josh muttered, moving to brush past her.

"Hold on." Andrea planted a palm against his chest. It felt like a brick wall. Her hand burned against him. Liquid warmth seeped through her muscles, robbing them of their readiness. Was she crazy? The guy could be in league with the man who attacked her and she was noticing his chest? Maybe she should be the one having her head examined. She swallowed hard and willed her muscles back into fight mode. "Why did you bring Wade here?"

"You're his counselor, I'm assuming? Alcohol abuse? He came to me and said he was struggling, that he'd slipped and started—"

"No." Andrea braced her free hand on the reception counter. History couldn't repeat itself. It couldn't. They'd worked too hard to set him free. "There's no way. Wade isn't using again. That's not possible." Wade Cameron had come so far. He'd shown up in her office with an alcohol addiction so strong he couldn't even get out of bed to go to physical training without a shot. When that didn't work, he'd turned to marijuana. One hit, and he knew he'd gone too far. That was the day he'd shown up in her office, begging for help, ready to break the craving that was dragging him to his knees through the muck, threatening to ruin his career.

Josh softened. "He asked for help. He has a lot of respect for you. Not too long ago, he told me if anything ever happened to him I should see his counselor, Andrea.

I had no problem bringing him here and waiting for him to come out again, only—"

"He never came out. But he never talked to me and there's no way he got out the back door."

Betrayal locked Josh's back teeth together, shooting pain through the muscles in his injured cheek. He should never have teamed up with her brother to teach her how to defend herself. He took two steps toward the closed closet.

Andrea pushed herself from the counter and grabbed his biceps. "No. Give him a chance to come out before you go barging in. If he's hiding, there's a reason. Let him man up and face you instead of dragging him out like a child."

Josh bit back a groan. Leave it to a therapist to play mind games. Fine. He'd call his soldier out, but he'd do it with every ounce of his authority. "Cameron!" The roar echoed off the walls.

Andrea jumped. "I didn't mean so loud," she muttered. "You make *me* want to hide in the closet."

With a quick, amused glance in her direction, Josh took a deep breath and swallowed some of his ire. If he were a scared kid, he wouldn't come out to bellowing, either. But any coward who hid while a lady fought off an attacker didn't deserve much leniency in his book. Still, he'd humor her and lower his voice, but he refused to tone down the sternness. "Let's go, Cameron. Time to talk."

No sound leaked from the closet.

"You scared him." Andrea wasn't smiling anymore. "Let me handle it." She stepped to the door. "Wade, it's Andrea Donovan. The only two people out here are me and First Sergeant Walker. It's safe."

When nothing happened, Josh's blood pressure soared. "This has gone far enough," he muttered, his words drowned out by sirens from an approaching police car.

Without wasting another second, he slipped around Andrea and yanked the wooden supply closet door open.

It was empty.

Wade Cameron had vanished.

TWO

When the front door to her apartment closed behind her, Andrea peered through the peephole and watched the policeman who had escorted her home disappear from sight down the heavy metal stairs. They'd searched her office building, taken her statement and Josh's, and insisted the paramedics give her a once-over. When they were finally convinced her ankle was only twisted and she'd been allowed to leave, the police had discovered Wade had crawled out through the drop ceiling to the office next door and walked out the back. The whole evening took on a surreal quality colored by a heightened emotional hangover and fatigue.

She turned and pressed her back against the door, staring at the empty space of an apartment that suddenly felt larger than the White House. What if the guy she'd kicked in the face had followed her home? What if he knew where she lived and was already here waiting?

Her spine dug into the door as she tried to make herself as small as possible. She'd chosen this apartment because its third-floor location meant the door was the only way in. Now, alone in the dark, only one way in meant only one way out. She'd been all bravado in front of Josh, confident after bruising her attacker, but being alone now seemed to make the day's events loom larger.

Josh. It had been years since she'd last seen him. He'd been her brother's high school baseball teammate, her first really big crush. The times he'd allowed his senior self to hang around a freshman like her, she'd have thought he'd dropped to one knee and proposed with a six-carat solitaire.

Andrea rolled her eyes heavenward and let them slip shut. *Lord Jesus, please don't let him remember the way I gushed over him back then.* That humiliation might be ten times worse than an attempted snatch and grab in her office lobby.

The feeling that unseen eyes watched her slowly dissipated as Andrea dropped the mail on the kitchen counter then marched through the apartment, flipping on lights and peeking in closets. Back in the kitchen, the neon of the microwave clock declared it to be nearly eleven. No wonder she was hungry enough to chew the linoleum like a puppy.

She dug a frozen chicken dinner out of the freezer and popped it into the microwave as a thought occurred to her. Puppies. Andrea had never been a dog person, but tonight it sure would be nice to have one. A dog would curl up beside her on the love seat and make her feel a little less alone. A dog would sound an alarm if someone tried to sneak in while sleep left her vulnerable.

Like sleep was going to happen anytime soon.

Every time she blinked, that giant of a man loomed in front of her. It wasn't hard to imagine what it would be like when she turned off the lights and actually shut her eyes. He'd likely materialize in her room and try to steal her again.

And this time, there would be no Josh Walker to intervene.

He'd taken her number with a promise to call if anyone found Wade Cameron, but she seriously doubted there would be a call from him otherwise. He'd barely said a personal word to her all evening. Even all these years later, that dredged up vague disappointment.

The beep of the microwave drowned out her chuckle. Guess some dreams never really died. Especially not the ones dreamed over melting ice cream and soft drinks with giggly girlfriends on warm spring days at high school baseball fields. Of course, the other girls were giggling over her brother. Back then it had been disgusting but now, with the haze of time to soften the edges of her memory, she could see where they'd found Brendan interesting. If only…

The shaking started again, but this time it came from the inside out, from the sudden rush of emotion at her brother's memory. The stainless-steel refrigerator door supported Andrea as she leaned back, trying to breathe through the internal assault. First the attack and now the memories. The army had taught her to keep a warrior's fist on her emotions, to kick fear into the nearest Iraqi canal. If an ambush on her convoy in the desert couldn't take her down, neither would a lone giant in her very own office.

With shaking hands, Andrea pulled the plastic tray from the microwave and grimaced at the contents, then dropped them into the trash. Peanut butter and jelly had to be better than this.

She was sloshing milk into a tall glass when her cell phone trilled. Nerves shook her hand and she stifled a groan as milk sloshed onto the mail she'd tossed to the counter earlier. Beautiful. It felt like the worst thing that could happen, the last nail in the coffin of a twisted day.

Andrea slammed the carton down and pinched the bridge of her nose. No way. She'd been through too much to morph into the girl who cried over spilled milk.

She snatched the phone from the counter and answered as she shoved envelopes away from the puddle of milk, streaking white across the dark stone. "Hello?" Her voice stretched as she reached for the towel hanging from the stove handle and mopped up the mess.

"Andrea?"

The deep timbre of the voice froze her hand in mid-swipe. Something about it made her heart take a side step, but it wasn't fear this time. It might be worse.

Cold milk seeped through the towel to her fingers, jolting her from her thoughts. "Oh!" Envelopes flew across the stovetop as she flicked her wrist in dismissal. "I mean, yes. It's me. Who is this?" Her mind wasn't sure, but her heart didn't have much doubt. Stupid memories.

There was a long pause from the other end of the line. "It's Josh Walker." His voice teetered slightly on the edge of uncertainty.

She'd just been wishing to hear his voice, just been wishing for the comfort of his presence. It was more than she'd thought it would be, washing a peace over her that defied description, the kind of peace she hadn't felt since… There was no way to remember when.

Distraction. There had to be a way to get away from the emotions his voice conjured. Nestling the phone in the crook of her neck, she gripped the nearest envelope and tore the end open. Even a credit card offer would be better than acknowledging she hadn't matured a whit since she was in high school. "Josh. How are you?" That was lame. She shook the envelope and let the contents slide into her hand, wishing life had a rewind button for moments like this.

Whatever Josh's answer was, it was drowned out by the sudden buzz in her ears. Staring up at her from the top photo in her hand was her own face as she spoke to the homeless man who often dropped by the office. Words, written in red ink, were scrawled across the image. *Stop what you're doing.* The image was taken through the scope of a rifle…and the crosshairs were centered on her forehead.

Josh's mind flashed giant red lights. "What's going on?" He sat up from where he'd flopped down on his couch as he'd dialed her number. Something had told him to call her. Had they found her? His feet hit the floor. "Did that guy—"

"No." The word was tight, like she'd wrapped it in rubber bands.

Something definitely wasn't right. "Talk to me, Andrea."

"Give me a second!" It was a whip shot straight to his gut. Either she didn't want to talk to him or very bad things were happening. Neither was good.

The silence nearly stretched on too long. "Someone sent me pictures." Andrea's voice held a measured control that did nothing to ease his mind. "Of me. At the counseling center. Two days ago." The pause seemed to crackle with her tension. "Through a high-powered scope."

Josh's back teeth ground together. He would not let this happen. He'd failed to act the last time, and the consequences still haunted him. This time would be different. "I'm coming over. Call the police, and I'll be there as—"

"Stop it." For the first time since she answered the phone, it didn't sound as if there was a script in front of her. "There's no reason for you to come here. All you can do is confirm for yourself that the photos exist."

"At least call the police."

"It's pointless. I managed to dump milk all over them before I touched them. Nobody's going to find anything." She sighed. "Realistically, what are they going to do? I've been through this with a client before. I'll have to keep the pictures and establish a pattern of harassment. And get a restraining order against…who? Nobody even knows who this guy is."

"There are emergency restraining orders."

"I know, but I'll be honest." She sniffed. "I can't take any more tonight. More police and more acknowledgement that this happened… It almost seems worse than the threat."

This wasn't something Andrea needed to dismiss so easily. If she planned to distance herself from anything, it shouldn't be the danger. And the way she was talking, she'd chosen ignorance over her own safety. "You're not considering the obvious." It was a bad move, whether or not he understood it. Too often overseas, he'd been tempted to lull himself into a false sense of security, to seek refuge in denial. But he'd watched one too many good soldiers die because he'd chosen the delusion of peace over the reality of imminent harm. Letting Andrea do the same wasn't part of his DNA.

"Believe me. I know. This isn't just about Wade's file. It might not even be about Wade at all. I don't know what to even consider. The thing I need most right now is to sleep and forget this is happening for a few hours, but we both know that probably won't happen."

He should hang up on her and call the police himself, but the likelihood of her forgiving him after that was pretty much nonexistent. If he severed ties with her, who would watch her back? If she wanted to go on her own, the least he could do was go with her. "Okay, against my better judgment, you can have your way. For now." Even as he said the words, second thoughts tore him apart. This went against all common sense. "But you have to let me do something."

The silence was long, and he let her have it. From what he remembered, pushing her was a guaranteed way to make her turn in on herself, like the armadillos that were so prevalent in the woods around Fort Benning. "What I need, I guess, is…to talk about something else. To be distracted. To not be alone."

Whatever cracked around his heart caused an almost physical pain. *Alone.* It was a feeling he knew all too well. He swallowed hard against what the sound of her voice did to his heart and sought for something to say. "You're really okay?" Why did his voice go four octaves deeper than usual?

He cleared his throat. It seemed like something had been stuck there ever since he climbed in his truck to drive home and realized he'd come face-to-face with Andrea Donovan again.

How could her unexpected appearance yank at something so deep inside him? He knew muscle memory was real. Years of training had proven it to him. Emotional memory was a new one. Apparently it existed, and it was strong. The things her voice did to him shouldn't happen this long after he'd last seen her, especially with all that had happened, but his skin prickled nonetheless.

"I'm okay." She took a breath so deep it echoed over the phone line. "I'm just really, really hungry."

Josh laughed so suddenly and so loudly it almost scared him. He just hoped she didn't think he was laughing at her.

To his relief, she joined him.

His immediate purpose drew into sharper focus. Right

now, Andrea needed him to do his best to fix this moment. "That sounded more like it should have been my line."

"It is what it is." She was clearly chewing. "Girls get hungry, too."

"And it sounds like they talk with their mouths full. So never call a guy a pig again. I know you've probably done it before. Every girl has."

She giggled, and the sound ran up his spine like lightning.

Josh dropped back onto the couch and stretched his feet out in front of him. The memory of her laughing as she watched her brother's baseball games played like a movie in front of him. It had been a challenge to keep his eye on the ball from third base. She'd flip her hair over her shoulder and throw her head back at something one of her friends said and, for a moment, he'd forget about base hits and ground balls. Yeah, she'd cost him an out or two back in the day.

The corner of his mouth tipped up. He'd forgive her.

It warmed him that she hadn't changed, that something of the girl he once knew still existed in the woman who'd stumbled back into his life today. What would it take to hear that laugh again? Back then he'd only enjoyed it from a distance. Every time they'd gotten close, she'd turned inside herself, grown quiet, the laughter disappearing from her eyes. Something about him had turned her so far off she ceased to be herself whenever he was around. Whatever it was, it seemed to have dissipated over the years. Josh took a deep breath and shook his head, trying to force the thoughts away. Frankly, he'd take what he could get. "What're you eating?"

"PB&J and a big ol' glass of milk." There was a pause, then her voice cleared after she swallowed. "Fighting for her life leaves a girl sort of hungry." The words didn't quite sound as light as she probably wanted them to.

The fear around the edges struck a nerve. More than anything, Josh wanted to slay that dragon for her. The only thing he could do from his couch was keep her talking. He scanned his living room as though a topic of conversation would suddenly appear. "So, you're a rehab counselor now?" He winced. That might keep her talking, but it wasn't a subject he necessarily wanted to broach.

"Substance abuse counselor. I was in the army for a while. I went in after Brendan…" Her voice weakened on her brother's name, but came back strong. "But then I decided I wanted to do something for the soldiers who are too afraid of having their careers destroyed if they go to army counseling or use Tricare to pay for services, so here I am working with soldiers and their families. Private donors and churches keep the doors open."

Her passion touched something deep inside him and sparked an appreciation she'd likely never understand. The desire to unload the whole story onto her nearly overwhelmed him, but he swallowed the words. She'd never forgive him, and he couldn't sever this tenuous bond now, not before he saw this to the end, protected now like he'd failed to protect so many years ago. "You see a lot of Brendan in these soldiers."

The line grew silent, the moments stretching so thin they almost groaned in protest. "Andrea?"

She sighed. "Especially in Wade."

His fingers tightened on the phone. This conversation wasn't going the way he'd intended, but he was in too deep now to pull out. "I'm sorry I wasn't at the funeral." He was. Sorrier than she knew. But he could never tell her why.

"I've heard it was a nice ceremony."

"You weren't there?"

"I was there." The sound of running water and the clink of glass on metal leaked through the phone, then silence. "I don't remember any of it. All I remember is anger. Everything's colored red, like there's a haze over it." Her voice was too matter-of-fact, too clinical.

There was no locating the source of the urge, but Josh knew he couldn't let her hide. "Anger at whom? Your brother?"

"Brendan, whoever got him started on heroin in the first place, his chain of command for not seeing it—"

"Yourself for not stopping it." Those thoughts never should have left his mouth, echoing guilt she was bound to hear. He cleared his throat. "He cared a lot about you, you know." *So did I.*

"I know." She sniffed. "You know what the hard part is? Not knowing. Did he do it on purpose or was that the one hit that was too much for his body to handle?"

"I think—" He stopped. Now was not the time for that discussion.

"I'm so done with thinking right now." Her voice dragged low, like the emotion gave added weight to the words.

What was going on in her head? Did she want to talk, or had she had enough of him for one day? His presence had to be a reminder of what she'd suffered. He'd err toward not making a pest of himself. "I'll let you go and eat. I'm sure you're starved after—"

"No. Don't."

Those short words he understood. "Anything wrong?"

The silence hung heavy. "I… Don't hang up yet, okay?"

Her request grabbed his heart in a fist. Never. After an appeal like that, there was no way he could. At the rate things were going, he'd likely never leave her alone again.

THREE

The midmorning sun baked the red brick of the counseling center and poured heat onto the brown metal roof of the eighties-era building. Reflected light bounced off the glass doors at an angle that obliterated the view into the lobby.

Andrea gripped the steering wheel so tightly her knuckles were the color of kindergarten paste. She twisted her fingers on the vinyl and squinted against the glare to see if anyone moved inside the building, but she could see nothing. She should have called Josh and asked him to meet her early, although that bordered on a paranoia she didn't want to acknowledge.

Acknowledged or not, it was there. The photos she'd received in the mail were safely at the police station, dropped off on her way to work this morning, but not before she'd photographed them with her phone. Andrea pulled up the most detailed image and studied it, trying to calculate the angle from which it was taken. Twisting to look over her shoulder, she scanned the wooded area across the street.

The trees were thick and dark, marking the line between Columbus and Fort Benning with thick pines and low-growing foliage. There were a thousand places to hide. Whoever took those photos could have walked into that undeveloped spot from anywhere, could have hidden behind any tree. Likely, there wouldn't be any witnesses. Worse… Was the person there even now, aiming at her again?

A shadow fell across the interior of her car as someone tapped on the driver window.

Andrea's shriek ricocheted off the windshield. She jumped sideways, away from the driver's-side door and the steely eyes of the man peering in.

"Doc, it's just me." The voice, colored in concern, drifted toward her on a wave of familiarity. A craggy, sun-weathered face peered into the window, a sunwashed black Dale Earnhardt baseball cap pulled low over faded blond hair and concerned gray-blue eyes. "You okay in there?"

Andrea swallowed a cry of relief. "Dutch." She pressed a hand to her chest to force her heart back into its rightful place.

The older man stepped back as she pushed the car door open and stepped out on shaky legs. He grasped her elbow to steady her as she gripped the top of the door and tried to find her wayward composure. "Didn't mean to scare you. Wanted to make sure you were okay."

Dutch had shown up in the parking lot of her building a couple of months ago, looking for work to help him get back on his feet. When the center grew busier as more units redeployed from overseas, he picked up the pace, showing up several days a week, right on schedule, to sweep the floors and neaten the parking lot. Andrea had no idea where he slept at night, but most of his days were spent drifting up and down this end of Victory Drive, rain or shine, picking up cans and bottles or helping shop owners with odd jobs.

"I'm fine. At least now that you're here." Thank God for Dutch. She'd all but forgotten it was Friday, one of his regular days to drop by.

Dutch slipped his cap back and scratched his hairline. "Whatcha mean by *now that I'm here?*"

Andrea jiggled the keys in her pocket and gripped her bag tighter as they neared the front of the building, only half hearing Dutch's question. At the door, she ran her hand over her name etched there, the tangible mark of a dream years in the making. There was no way she'd let a hulking monster with a camera scare her away from her calling.

Still, as she stared through the glass at the lobby floor where she'd clawed desperately for freedom last night, her stomach tightened. It had seemed like a million miles across that floor at the time, but it was more like two feet in reality. It was amazing how fear could wreak havoc on perception.

"Doc?" Dutch's deep Southern drawl drew her out of the vision of angry eyes and a menacing figure.

The keys jingled like bells as she pulled them from her pocket. "It's nothing." It took all of her strength to keep her hand from trembling as she unlocked the door. Once they were inside, half the battle was over. She'd done it. Crossed the threshold and not lost her senses doing it. Still, nothing could stop her from staring back through the window at the trees.

"Well, now." Dutch glanced around the exposed lobby, pulling on his earlobe. "Looks like you don't—" He stopped, eyes focused on the floor, head tipped to one side.

"What's the matter?" Andrea followed his gaze and instantly landed on what had caught his attention.

"What is that?" Dutch knelt and studied the rust-colored smudges near the door. "Is that blood?" His head came up, jaw set. "Did somebody hurt you?" He stood and squared off as though prepared to protect her from giant robots.

"I'm fine." She forced nonchalance into her voice. "If you want to know the truth, I drew that blood."

Dutch took a step back. "What did you do? I'm not 'bout to be in here mopping up evidence, am I?"

Laughter bubbled up at the suspicion in his stance. "I didn't kill one of my patients, if that's what you're thinking. And the police have come and gone, so you can do whatever you'd like."

"Well, if it's not your blood, then whose is it?" He didn't quite believe her.

"I wish I knew. A man came in here and tried to take one of my files." *And me, if he could.* She dared not say that aloud. She might find herself with a homeless man as a permanent bodyguard. "I kicked him in the face and he left."

"One of your patient files? Which one?"

"You know I can't tell you who my clients are."

For a moment, it seemed he was going to ask again, then he changed course. "You kicked a man in the teeth? Was he a big guy?"

"Huge."

"Always knew you had scrap in you, Doc." Dutch chuckled and headed for the supply room, shaking his head. "You can take care of yourself, can't you?"

Yes, she could. But that was something she didn't want to have to prove again soon.

The door opened, scraping adrenaline against her raw nerves. That had to stop, or she'd fall to pieces.

A short, balding man stepped in, his purple uniform polo tucked into too-tight khaki pants. "Miss Andrea." He extended a disposable cup of coffee to her.

She took the cup and smiled, the warmth of fresh-brewed coffee seeping into her fingers, up her arm and into her soul. Every morning, Mr. Miller stepped in right behind her with a cup of coffee and a dose of cheer. Just when she thought she was alone in this, God reminded her she had people looking out for her. "Mr. Miller. Always faithful with the coffee."

"Always." His grin nearly split his round face in two before it faded and he jerked his thumb over his shoulder toward his gas station next door. "My evening shift guy says he saw the police over here last night. You okay?"

"She kicked a man in the teeth," Dutch called from the supply room.

Mr. Miller took a step back and nearly fell out the door as it opened again.

Josh slipped in behind the smaller man, nodding at her as he did.

This time, when her fingers tingled, it had nothing to do with fear. That needed to stop, too.

Glancing at Josh, Mr. Miller recovered his footing and stepped sideways from the man who was his physical opposite. Then he looked back at Andrea. "You kicked a man in the teeth?"

Josh chuckled, but that only made Mr. Miller glance back and forth between the two of them.

Dutch reappeared and started when he saw Josh. "Who are you?" The way he gripped the broom handle, it looked like he might just charge.

Andrea held up her hands, hoping to head off any misplaced protection. "Okay, everybody. I'm not used to three handsome men in my lobby at once." Especially one in particular.

As if he knew what she was thinking, Josh winked at her.

Please, Lord, now is not the time to blush. She cleared

her throat, made introductions then took charge of her small band of defenders. "Mr. Miller, I'm okay. Someone tried to rob me, but it's fine now. The police are looking into it. Hopefully, it was an isolated incident." Hopefully. But she doubted it. So did Josh, based on the set of his jaw.

Mr. Miller studied her as Dutch went back to sweeping in the corner. "Maybe I should aim a few of my security cameras your way. Make sure there's always eyes on the place." He nodded. "I'll have all of my shifts keep an eye out for anything suspicious."

"You don't have to do that."

"I do." He laid a hand on her arm, which made Josh straighten slightly. Like he should be jealous of someone old enough to be her father. "I want to. Having you next door is so much nicer than having that check-cashing place here gouging soldiers." He patted her arm, aimed a slight smile at Josh, then stepped for the door. "I should go. It's payroll day." He nodded at Dutch. "You coming to my place next?"

Dutch tossed a slight wave from where he leaned on his broom handle. "An hour or so?"

With an answering wave, Mr. Miller tripped on the threshold as he stepped out. "See you on Monday, Ms. Andrea."

Josh arched an eyebrow.

Yes, Mr. Miller was awkward, but nobody treated her better. Except maybe Dutch. Her forehead wrinkled. She certainly had eclectic neighbors. "What brings you by so early?" she asked Josh. "Don't you have to work?"

"Command gave us a four-day weekend now because we were doing an extended training exercise over the Fourth of July holiday."

"Convenient." Andrea let herself meet his eyes and wished she hadn't. Something about him blurred the straight edges of her life until she wasn't quite sure if she was fifteen or thirty-two.

"Still don't know who you are." Dutch's broom ceased its swishing as he drew closer.

Josh extended his hand. "Josh Walker."

"Dutch."

The men sized each other up as they shook, seemed to come to some agreement and parted.

Dutch drifted back to the closet and reappeared seconds later, sans broom. "Think I'll go see what Mr. Miller needs. You two look like you need to talk." Without further explanation, he slipped out the door.

"What was that?" Andrea asked as she led Josh into her office and watched as he took in the room.

"What?"

"That. Between you and Dutch."

"Guy conversation."

"So you're friends now?"

"For life." Josh grinned and leaned against her desk, his smile fading. "How long have you known him?"

Andrea sucked her upper lip between her teeth and studied the popcorn ceiling. Odd time to think of it, but she should have removed that before she moved in. "A couple of months. He does odd jobs for several businesses on Victory. For Mr. Miller, too."

"And how long have you known Miller?"

"Since I moved in. Six months or so." She tipped her coffee cup toward Josh. "Every day, like clockwork, he brings me coffee from his gas station next door. Why?" But even as she said it, she knew. "You suspect them?"

"I think everybody's up to something right now. Don't you?"

She hadn't thought about it. "No. And especially not them." Rounding her desk, she dropped into her chair and waited for him to sit in one across from her. "Have you stopped to think you're the most likely suspect?" She unlocked the desk drawer and grabbed Wade's file, slipping it onto the desk like it was explosive. And who knew? It might be.

"I have." He nodded toward the folder. "You left that here last night? Unguarded?"

"Safest place for it. The police were here and, for all anyone knew, they were watching." She flipped open the folder and stared down at the first page. It was easier than looking at Josh.

"You took the pictures to the police?"

She nodded, flipping through the folder to find Wade's release of information form. Last night she'd realized that talking to the person he trusted the most—the one to whom he'd given permission to access his patient information—might yield a clue. It was a sheet she rarely glanced at, because it only supplied clerical details.

Her finger stilled when she located the form, then tapped the name penned there in Wade's precise handwriting. What exactly was going on here?

"What is it?"

Andrea's face paled and her eyebrows drew together so tightly they had to make her forehead ache.

Closing the file, she tapped the corner against her desk blotter. "You brought Wade here because he wanted help. But you also said Wade told you to come here if anything ever happened to him. Don't you find that odd?"

"Guys coming and going from deployment say a lot of things like that."

She shook her head, then held the folder out to him.

It was a fight to keep his face neutral as he grasped the thick packet, careful not to get his fingers anywhere near hers. The last thing he needed was to touch her and set crazy thoughts to racing again.

The manila folder lay heavy in his hands, the name *Cameron, Wade* typed neatly on a tab above what he assumed was a reference number. "Why give this to me?"

"Open it."

"I can't look at this, and you know it." Heat flushed Josh's face. He wasn't a therapist or a lawyer, but everyone knew about confidentiality between a counselor and a patient. The idea that Andrea would breach that for any reason plummeted his respect for her about seven pegs, and with that drop came a sense of disappointment deeper than any he should feel. He stood and dropped the folder on her desk, ignoring her confusion. "You could have your license yanked for violating confidentiality." Which presented a whole other dilemma for him. Did he tell someone? Or did he protect her?

"Sit down, Josh." Her tone held authority and maybe even anger. "I should hope you'd know me better than that." With a flick of her wrist, she flipped open the file, paged through, and jammed her finger onto a printed sheet. "Wade cleared you as the only other person who could put eyes on his file."

Everything froze. Even the small clock on a low cherry bookshelf seemed to tick slower. "Why would Cameron choose me? I'm nobody to the kid, other than his first sergeant. There's every reason *not* to want his chain of command to be given access to his records. In certain instances, what's in here could wreck his career. It doesn't make sense." Josh sank into the chair and slid the file closer, scanning the release of records form and noting the slash through a previous name and his name etched in its place with precise print. "You're sure he did this?"

"I'm no handwriting analyst, but he's the one who filled

out all of the other paperwork, and the handwriting all seems to be the same."

"Why?"

"Couldn't tell you. He never once mentioned you in any of his sessions. I'd have remembered hearing your name if he had."

She'd have recognized his name, just like he'd have known hers anywhere. Did that mean she'd given him more than a passing thought over the years? Josh shook his head. That would be way too much to hope.

Andrea blushed a deep red and straightened a few pens on her desk into a neat row before she cleared her throat. "I never give the administrative pages more than a cursory glance, because that's more up Grace's alley. My receptionist. It's the stuff she enters into the computer, and unless there's a reason, I prefer not to go digging there. It can color my judgments, make me jump to conclusions."

"So you just now noticed?"

She looked startled at the straightforward question, like it wasn't the direction she'd expected him to go. "This is the first time I've opened the file in a couple of months. For some reason, he gave you permission to look into it. That makes you the only other eyes I have, because unless he's threatened to hurt himself or someone else or the authorities bring me a court order, nobody else can see it." She tapped a finger on the edge of her desk. "It's just me and you on this."

The folder nearly slipped from his fingers. It almost sounded as if the words meant more than they sounded like on the surface.

Great. Now his mind was playing tricks on him. He couldn't get lost in the subtext of every word she said—not if he had any chance of protecting her. He hoped there wouldn't be more danger, but something in his gut wouldn't quiet down. It was a sixth sense developed over four tours overseas, and it had never done him wrong before.

What he needed was distance, to get out of her presence, to put his head on straight before he did something stupid like lean across that desk and kiss her.

Because that wouldn't help matters at all.

"I'm guessing I can't take this home with me." Josh tried to keep the hope out of his voice.

"'Fraid not. I'm not so all-fire sure this is about anything in there, not after getting those pictures, but our visitor last night was a little too hot to get his hands on that file, which makes it the only hope I have of finding out what's going on here. It's not leaving my sight."

"You're planning to keep it with you?" His fight response marched double-time. Didn't she know how stupid that was? "All it takes is someone to track you down—"

"And what? If anybody wants it that badly, they'll break in here first. Since they didn't try last night, it adds credence to my doubts about what they're really after." She crossed her arms over her chest and leaned back in the burgundy leather chair. "Like I already said, that file's a cover for something else. Something to do with me." Her voice wavered on that last sentence. Andrea might be all bravado up front, but the memory of what had happened—and probably of what could happen—frightened her. It was clear she didn't want him to know that, though.

"Let me keep it." Josh gripped the folder so tightly the cardstock popped in protest. "They'll never suspect—"

Andrea rocketed out of her chair like she intended to come across the desk and snatch the file from his hands. "You're not listening to me. Is this the typical 'hero' tactic? Do you play movies in your head while women speak so you don't have to hear what we say? It's clear from those pictures they will come after me regardless. You putting yourself in the middle of this any more than you already are only puts you in danger, too."

"I'm not going anywhere." There was no way Andrea would ever understand what drove him. And he sure wasn't about to tell her now. She'd break even the tenuous tie that bound them and never speak to him again.

"I don't doubt that. But I also don't intend to let you get caught in the crossfire."

He gripped the file and stood, looking down at her, his throat tight with emotions he couldn't define, though exasperation was probably highest on the list. "Too late." Without looking back, he stalked to the door and vanished into the lobby.

Andrea glanced at her cell phone and winced. Nearly lunchtime. With Grace on vacation, she'd made the calls to her Friday appointments and canceled them last night, unsure if anyone would even be allowed in the building today. With no sessions, the day dragged on without mercy. It had been a vain hope that patient-free time would let her catch up on paperwork, but yesterday's stress had scattered her thinking and twisted her mind to such an extent that even the smallest task took an eternity to complete.

It didn't help that Josh had stormed out of her office over two hours ago, carried by emotions she couldn't begin to puzzle out.

Okay, maybe he hadn't exactly stormed out, but the rigid line of his spine and the complete silence of his exit spoke more than shouts ever would. As much as she'd replayed their conversation, she couldn't figure out exactly what would cause that kind of reaction. Yes, she'd been stubborn, but that didn't warrant his response.

She knew the only reason he was still in the lobby was because he'd never leave with that file, no matter how hot his anger simmered. He might disagree with her, but something told her he had the same integrity as always. She'd expected him to duck back in with something. A comment on Wade's file, an apology for his strange behavior, a question about lunch… But nothing. Two hours and nothing.

Analyzing that man was half of the reason her paperwork had dragged on so long. No matter how hard she tried, she couldn't ignore the pull of his presence just a few feet away, on the other side of a door that might as well be made of lead.

A familiar low hum pulsed into the room. It took a moment for Andrea to place the sound, and when it processed, she whirled as a sheet slipped into the wireless printer. The wheels on her chair squeaked as she rolled backward. Josh couldn't have logged into Grace's computer without a password, so who was printing on her machine?

Slowly, an image formed. Andrea and Dutch, standing by her car. This morning. The photo was taken this time through a car windshield from one of the parking lots to the west of the center.

Again, red words were scrawled across the photo. *We're still watching.*

She drew in a sharp breath and willed her fingers not to shake as she pulled the paper from the machine.

Andrea shoved her chair back and stood, every cell focused on that photo. "Josh?"

No answer.

Spider steps of fear ran up her arms. Not knowing what was happening on the other side of the door made her body tense. She swallowed hard and shook off the irrational thought that someone had slipped in and murdered Josh while she worked only feet away. Things like that didn't happen outside of horror movies. Or war zones. Even though her life felt like both right now, that couldn't possibly happen. "Josh? They sent another picture." That should get his attention.

Still nothing. No rustle of movement. No answering call. It was as still as if she were alone in the world.

Something was definitely wrong. Andrea edged toward the door and gathered her last ounce of courage, ignoring the pounding of her heart as it throbbed in her ears. As softly as possible, she eased the door open, keeping out of sight from the windows in the lobby, trying to catch a glimpse of Josh.

The midday sun, nearly straight overhead, bounced off the windshield of her car in the parking lot, reflecting on the glass in the lobby and casting shadows that wavered in the heat. Josh sat at Grace's desk with his arms crossed, just out of reach of the brightest streaks, his forehead resting on his palms, seemingly absorbed in the file in front of him. From this angle, though, she could see that his eyes weren't on the pages but focused on the front windows.

Josh glanced to the side when she appeared in the doorway. "Stay there," he hissed.

Andrea blinked against the adrenaline that shot through her from her scalp to her toes. "What's wrong?"

"Hopefully nothing." Josh shifted, raised his head and stretched, rubbing the back of his neck. He ran his hand down his face to block his mouth. "Truck pulled up in the parking lot about three minutes ago."

"Did you call the police?"

"Not yet. I don't want to tip them off that I—" His entire body tensed, his fingers tightening on his face. "Go in your office. Lock the door. Now."

"But—"

"Someone's coming. Now!"

The whispered shout galvanized her. Without waiting to see what came next, Andrea slammed the door and pushed the lock, then looked around the room and lunged for the phone on her desk.

There were no windows to see what was happening. No portal through which to escape. Her adrenaline-numbed fingers fumbled the handset of her desk phone.

No way out. She had no way out.

And she'd left Josh at the mercy of a potential killer.

FOUR

As soon as the lock clicked on Andrea's door, Josh abandoned all pretense. He'd had plenty of time to settle on a course of action and to determine that there was only one choice. He was wide-open and in full view in the lobby, and if the guy had a gun, the windows wouldn't save him.

If he was going to die, he was going to go down fighting.

Josh gauged the man's approach and watched him hesitate at the sidewalk. It seemed he noticed Josh for the first time and wasn't sure what to make of his unexpected presence.

The man's stance was familiar. So was the face.

"Andrea!" he called over his shoulder. "Don't call the police!"

Josh vaulted the reception desk and rushed for the door as the man turned to run. It seemed to take an eternity to cross the lobby and enter the parking lot, but in a race of quick strides, he caught the man by the arm just before he reached the small pickup truck. "Cameron. Don't."

Wade Cameron's eyes flashed wild with emotion that looked more like anger than the fear Josh expected. His mouth opened, then closed as his eyes narrowed and his fists balled.

With a quick glance around the parking lot, Josh jerked the younger man toward the door, trying to get him out of the line of fire in case a shooter was watching. While they hadn't determined who was in the most danger, Josh knew Wade probably had a target on his back the size of a stop sign.

Josh yanked the door open to find Andrea standing in the open doorway to her office.

She gasped when she saw who he dragged with him. Her hands went to her mouth. "Wade? What are you doing here?"

Andrea stepped aside as Josh hauled Wade into her office, away from the windows of the lobby. Once inside, he dropped Wade into a chair like a rag doll and stood over him, staring down like he intended to chew the boy up and spit him out. "Have you lost your mind coming here, Cameron?"

It had been years since Andrea had stared down an angry first sergeant. She was more than happy not to be on the receiving end of that glare now.

"Do you have any idea what happened after you vanished yesterday?" Josh leaned into Wade's personal space. "Where have you been?"

Wade sank so far against the back of the chair that it was a wonder he didn't slip right through it.

Andrea swallowed hard and gripped her hands behind her back. She wouldn't step in, even though everything in her wanted to. There was still too much army in her blood to allow her to question a first sergeant.

As if Josh could read her thoughts, he straightened and paced to the door. He ran his hand across the short hair on the top of his head and gripped the back of his neck as he stared into the lobby.

He could be counting to ten. Or twenty. Or more, if the square of his shoulders was any indication.

"Andrea?" Wade's low voice drew her.

In all the times she'd counseled Wade, even in the deepest discussions about his past, he'd never looked so much like a scared child as he did right now. He radiated fear, almost shrinking inside his jeans and dark red T-shirt.

Red. Not the greatest color to wear when you were already a target.

Andrea sank in her chair beside him and tried to make the scene as familiar as possible. He'd probably come here looking for a safe place, and she had no choice but to help him. "What's going on, Wade?"

"Is First Sergeant Walker going to hurt me?"

"I doubt it. He'd get in way too much trouble if he did."

"It'd cost me my career," Josh muttered from the doorway, his focus never leaving the front lobby.

He was pulling security, keeping watch to make sure no one crept up on them. The fact hit Andrea square in the chest. Whoever had attacked her yesterday knew Wade had been here. What were the chances someone was watching to see if he came back?

A shudder shook her before she found her center. Whatever was going on, the answer sat in front of her, and scaring him into flight would get them nowhere. She assumed a soothing voice. "Why did you come here yesterday just to run away?"

Wade's hands clenched and unclenched around the arm of the chair. "Can we..." His anxious gaze took in every inch of the room except the space where she sat. "Can we talk out front?"

"No."

The stern denial from Josh was enough to strike fear into Andrea's heart. Wade would never open up under that kind of duress. "We'd be wide open out there. In here, nobody can see you." She shifted in her chair. "Now, what made you run away?"

Wade didn't seem to hear her.

Josh looked over his shoulder and caught Andrea's eye. She hoped he could read her plea for help. If they didn't get him to talk they were no better off than when he was missing.

"Answer her, Cameron." He barked the order then turned away, obviously confident that his soldier would obey.

It sure didn't seem that way. The look of anger and fear that raced across Wade's face sent a shudder down Andrea's spine. For a guy who trusted his first sergeant enough to make him a point of contact and a rightful observer of his counseling files, Wade didn't seem to like Josh very much. "We have to talk out there."

"No, we don't." The tone behind her words brooked no argument.

For the sparest instant, Wade tensed like he was going to lunge for the door. As quick as the stance appeared, it evaporated. Wade loosened his grip on the chair and tilted his head to stare at the floor in front of the desk, sheer resignation covering his features. "He told you, didn't he? Why I made him bring me here?"

"You started drinking again." Andrea's muscles tensed.

"I'm sorry. I didn't want to. I had it cold. I had it beat, then..." His chin dropped to his chest. "They kept pressuring me. And I fell."

"Who was pressuring you?" Josh's voice was hard, but Andrea couldn't tell what the emotion was behind it. Anger, fear and sorrow all warred in those words.

"*They* were!" Wade balled his fists. He bolted from the chair, an iron rod of unleashed fury focused solely on

Josh. "I can't *tell* you. Okay? It was them!" He whipped toward Andrea, but his eyes focused past her at the wall behind her desk before his shoulders slumped. "It's so much more than you think."

The words plunged through Andrea's chest and gripped her heart so tightly she had to struggle for another breath. Everything about Wade's behavior drew into sharp focus even as the room around them seemed to fade. "You're using. And it's stronger than alcohol."

Wade jerked his head back to stare at the ceiling. His breathing slowed, and once again he sat in the chair, leaning forward and pressing his hands into his close-cropped hair. "Heroin."

The room whirled like a carnival ride. *Heroin.* The same monster that had ripped her brother out of this world. How could he? How could he know her pain and still fall prey? She'd poured her heart and soul into him. Believed in him. Trusted that it was safe for Wade to step down from counseling and simply go to meetings with his sponsor.

She'd been wrong. She'd missed something big. She'd failed both of them.

"Andrea." Josh's voice cut through the anger and grief, but it wasn't until he said it the second time that she lifted her head.

He still stood in the doorway, dividing his attention between her and the world outside. It was hard to tell from here if he was angry at Wade or feeling sorry for her, but neither was something she could handle.

"This is not about you."

Momentary rage swelled in her. This was so about her, about Brendan, about…

One glance at Cameron's broken countenance stopped the tide of self-pity. Her shoulders squared. Josh was right.

She could grieve for her brother and berate herself for her failure later. Right now, the young man in front of her needed her full attention. She forced her muscles to untighten. *One second at a time.* "What happened?"

"Can't we talk about this out front?"

A sharp gesture from Josh dismissed the recurring question. "You'll leave this room when I say so. Now, answer her question."

"Wade." Andrea slid her chair forward, bringing herself next to her former patient. She wanted to repeat the original question, but it was clear he wasn't going to answer. Someone was watching Wade and her. The two of them in the same room was bound to be a temptation that couldn't be resisted for long. As much as she ached for Wade, she needed answers, to know who had attacked her. It seemed there was no way to get Wade to talk without coaxing him step by step, so she started at the beginning. "Why did you come here yesterday?"

"I didn't know where else to go."

From where he stood looking out into the lobby Josh asked, "And why run?"

Wade ran his hands down his thighs, gripping his knees. "I got here and realized how much trouble I could be in with you and that I couldn't—"

"Not buying it."

Andrea silently urged Josh to back off, but he either wasn't receiving the message or he didn't care. Something about Wade's confession had stiffened his backbone and hardened his countenance. There would be no more pity.

Wade sat forward like he was going to leap up again, then settled back into his seat. "My…dealer. He saw me when I came in. He pulled into the parking lot of the gas station next door." He looked up and met Andrea's eyes, telegraphing fear. "I didn't know what else to do. I wasn't about to grab the phone, dial the police and ask for help because my drug suppliers are breathing down my neck."

"They wanted a look at your file." Andrea gauged Wade's reaction to see if any of her words hit a raw nerve.

He tugged at his shirt collar. "Please, Andrea. The lobby. It's claustrophobic in here. I can't breathe."

Had Wade Cameron developed a phobia on top of his slide past the bottle into drugs? "You're not telling me something."

Wade sucked in a deep breath. "My file." The words held a note of resignation. "I put something in it they don't want you to see. You have to give it to me or—"

"Are we supposed to believe this?" Josh's voice came low across the room. "You aren't making any sense. Do you owe these guys money?"

"Not exactly."

The hesitation in the denial sapped the last of Andrea's strength. She gripped the edge of her desk, feeling the situation spin further and further out of control. "You were selling." The words brought bile into the back of her throat with them. For a panicked second, she thought she'd have to dive for the trash can under her desk, but a deep breath and a slow count to ten stopped the room from spinning.

"No." Wade shook his head, panic coloring his expression. "I...I knew what they were doing and I wanted to stop them, so I got them to let me start moving product for them."

"Oh, yeah. That's so much better than selling." Josh's utter lack of respect weighted the air in the room.

At the moment, Andrea didn't have the heart to reprimand him. She felt the same level of disgust, although hers was aimed more at herself than at the kid in front of her. If she'd handled his case right from the start and seen the signs, he wouldn't be in this situation now, so messed up that he talked in riddles and circles.

Wade seemed to read their thoughts. He slid forward in the chair. "You're getting it all wrong. They wanted me to do things I didn't want to do, so I took their stuff. I hid it. I never delivered it. And now…"

"Now they're after you?" Andrea choked on fear for Wade. "What were you thinking? Why didn't you go to the cops?"

"You went vigilante, Cameron?" It was hard to tell if Josh's words held anger or respect.

"I just wanted to stop them from sucking more of your soldiers in. It's too late for me, but I wanted to keep them from…" Wade broke into a coughing fit so hard his face turned red. "But it turns out these aren't local Columbus or Phenix City guys." He choked, sputtered then gained control. "These guys are capable of way more than I thought. I can't win. I can't save—"

At the door, Josh straightened and dropped his hands to his sides, the movement shaking Wade out of his confession.

Andrea's senses leaped into high alert, adrenaline striking her heart. "What do you see?"

"They're here, aren't they?" Wade's voice sounded flat, not agitated or alarmed as she'd have expected. "They heard me. I said too much." He slumped in the chair, apparently resigned that this was his end.

Josh pressed his lips together and didn't answer for a second. "Somebody's here. A car drove through the parking lot and slowed down. Just hang tight."

Keys shook on the ring as Andrea snatched them from the desk drawer. "We can go out the back."

"Last resort." Josh shook his head as Wade stood. "We

don't know who's back there. Andrea, get ready to dial 911."

For the second time in an hour, Andrea gripped the desk phone and prepared to make the kind of call that only happened in nightmares. But when she pulled it to her ear, she heard nothing. "It's dead."

"We're not getting out," Wade muttered, slipping out of his chair to his knees.

Josh pointed at her desk. "Use your cell."

It took a second for her fear-gripped muscles to respond. It was like she was under water, and she couldn't breathe, couldn't move fast enough through the resistance. Everything slowed down, and her senses took it all in. The ticking of the clock on her desk, the rasp of Wade's breathing.

As her fingers brushed the rugged case of her cell phone, time slipped back to normal. A split second later Josh dove for the floor and shouted, "Get down!"

Overlaying the command was the crack of a gunshot, the sound of breaking glass and Andrea's own screams.

The SUV's tires squealed against the pavement as Josh propped himself on his elbows and peered around the door. Glass littered the floor from the shattered front door, the top panel obliterated.

As the vehicle whipped out of the parking lot, Josh scrambled up, throwing aside self-preservation, and rushed into the parking lot, trying to identify the SUV or the driver, but he wasn't fast enough. The vehicle was off in the direction of 185, swallowed by traffic.

If the glass wasn't already broken, he'd have put his fist through it.

Even though he knew Andrea was okay, he turned on his heel to go check on her, to see for himself that some megabullet hadn't pierced the interior walls and hit her in her office. As he pulled the door open, he traced the path of the round that had destroyed the glass. The mirror over the reception desk hung crooked, glass lying in jagged pieces on the bookcase beneath it.

"The message couldn't be any clearer, could it?" Andrea's voice came from her office door.

Josh turned, wishing he'd moved faster, had somehow caught the shooter in the parking lot. "Message?"

"That bullet took out the door glass, the only glass in the building that had my name on it. That's no coincidence. They aren't kidding about me shutting down."

Biting back words he knew he shouldn't say, he pulled her into the office. "Maybe you should listen to them, at least until this blows over. If this is really about shutting you down, then giving them what they want, even temporarily—"

Cameron rose slowly from where he'd taken a dive behind the chair in front of the desk. "Are they gone?"

Biting back words Josh knew he shouldn't say, he swallowed silent anger at the interruption. Then one glance at Andrea's face, stormy with anger, and he decided it might be better this way. If he'd said much more, she might have taken another swipe at him. Knowing her, she wasn't going anywhere, threats or not. He addressed Cameron instead. "They're gone."

"I should have seen this coming." Andrea snatched a piece of paper from her desk. "And I'm not shutting down. Even temporarily. I refuse to run. What would happen if I did?" She held the paper out with a rustle.

The edges wrinkled in his grip. "When was this taken?"

"This morning. They sent it to my printer. It's wireless. Somehow..."

Josh wanted nothing more than to cross the room and pull her into his arms, to let her know he'd shelter her no matter what happened. But he couldn't. He couldn't make a promise to protect her, and he couldn't let himself want her in the irrational way he did right now. He was starting to think he needed the services of a counselor more than he ever had before.

Rather than think any more about that, he dropped the photo to the desk and yanked his phone from his pocket, dialing 911.

"What are you doing?" Wade seemed to grow two inches taller as his spine straightened.

Had he really asked that question? "Calling the police. There was a shooting here, remember?"

"You can't call the police. That will make everything worse. Everything." Cameron stepped closer. "First Sergeant, I'm begging you not to do that."

Josh refused to take a step back from the kid. He telegraphed a silent warning to Andrea, then motioned her forward and passed her the phone. As soon as he knew the operator was on the line, he edged closer, toe-to-toe with the young soldier who was quaking more by the moment. "And how is Andrea supposed to explain the bullet hole in her wall? It's too late. They'll find out whether we tell them or not. Guns don't get fired at buildings without someone noticing."

"Nobody's going to call the police. Not around here."

"What's so menacing around here that no one would call the cops?" As more time passed, he trusted Cameron less and less. Something undefinable muddied the air in the room, and it originated with the young soldier in front of him. "What's really going on?"

Andrea stepped up beside him. "They're on the way."

Sheer terror slipped a veil over Wade Cameron's face.

"They know. Everything." He shook his head and dug his fingers into his thighs. "And they'll be back."

"Everything about what?" Before Josh fully formed the words, Cameron leaped forward and shoved Andrea to the side.

Josh could only watch as her back crashed into the wall with so much force that she bounced off, hitting the floor on her hands and knees, gasping for air.

Cameron hesitated before he took advantage of the distraction and bolted past Josh, out of the office and into the afternoon heat. It took a split second for Josh to process all of the motion and to react.

It was enough time to put him at a disadvantage. He was barely out the door before the truck roared to life and spun out of the parking lot.

But this time he was able to get a license plate number.

He recited it over and over as he raced back into the office to check on Andrea. If she was hurt… If he'd let harm come to her while he stood there and watched…

When he tore back into the office, she was settling back on the floor, sucking in deep breath after deep breath. Her head came up when he entered. "Fine. I'm fine."

Josh knelt beside her and once again fought the urge to pull her to him. "Really?"

"Yeah. Got the air knocked out of me, that's all." She pulled in another breath and held it like she was trying to force her body into some sense of rhythm, her face white but regaining color as he watched. "Why'd he run?"

"Because you called the cops and he's using?" Josh rocked back on his heels to put distance between them before he did something supremely out of place and stupid. "I don't know. But everything makes less sense now than it did before." He pressed his hands against his thighs and stood, his elbow aching in old accusation. He battled the urge to go off and handle all of this by himself. Instead, he strode to the door and stared across the parking lot, listening as the faint sound of distant sirens drew closer.

Andrea watched him for a moment, then gripped the edge of her desk and pulled herself to her feet, wincing as she did. "What happens next?"

"The cops couldn't look for Cameron before because he took off on his own, but they can sure go after him now."

"For what?"

"Assault." A police car raced into the parking lot, another close behind. "One way or another, they're going to bring him in this time."

FIVE

Andrea rubbed the corner of one eye with her index finger and dropped her fork onto her paper plate of fast-food Chinese orange chicken, too exhausted to chew another bite. Admitting defeat, she sat back and stared across the table at Josh.

"You look like death warmed over." He popped a French fry into his mouth and eyed her. "Did you sleep at all last night?"

"Not until early this morning." After yesterday's shooting she'd wandered the apartment wrapped in a sweater, too scared to close her eyes. Just before 3:00 a.m., she'd dared to peek out the window and spotted Josh's truck in the parking lot, at the end of a line of trees where he likely believed he was hidden. The thought that she should invite him up or at least take him a cup of coffee had crossed her mind, but the next thing she knew, it was daylight, and she was sprawled out on the oversize chair in her alcove, her body protesting a sleep position she hadn't attempted since college.

Today, neither of them had mentioned his vigil. But it wasn't fair that he looked wide awake and gorgeous while she looked like a new recruit after week one of basic.

Yeah, she'd seen herself in the mirror this morning. It was a wonder Josh hadn't lost his appetite.

The large room hummed around them as diners searched for tables and shoppers sought bargains in the small stores that lined the wall opposite the fast-food counters. In hindsight, the food court at the Post Exchange on the Saturday of a payday weekend probably hadn't been the wisest of choices for lunch, but the activity gave her something to focus on other than her thoughts.

After a lengthy discussion with the police while Mr. Miller and Josh boarded up the remnants of her front door, then a nearly sleepless night spent staring into shadows, Andrea definitely needed this outlet. When Josh had called at ten and offered to take her to lunch, she'd jumped at the chance to avoid more pacing in her apartment. And, if she had to be honest, to spend more time with him.

This was getting dangerous, and not just because she seemed to be a marked target. There were her former unhealthy feelings for Josh Walker to contend with, also. Still, that didn't stop her from being grateful he was here now.

Josh sipped a long draw on his soda before he settled his cup on the table, clearly more awake than Andrea could ever dream of being.

Speaking of that…Andrea thunked the side of her brown plastic tray. She had thought she'd keep her knowledge of Josh's nighttime vigil a secret, but the fact that he looked so refreshed just wouldn't let her. "How do you do it?"

"Do what? Eat them like this?" He slathered a French fry in mustard and held it out to her. "I learned it from a buddy in Germany. You should try it."

She batted his hand away. Mustard wouldn't cross her lips if it was the last condiment on earth.

"That's right." He nodded with a grin. "You don't eat mustard. Guess I forgot."

The fact that he remembered at all was enough to make her woozy. She cleared her throat. *Focus.* "No. How do you stay up all night and still look like you do today?"

The mustarded fry hesitated halfway to his mouth, then he popped it in with one smooth motion. "What makes you think I did anything other than sleep like a baby?"

Andrea swirled her fork through a pile of fried rice. Maybe she was wrong. Maybe that was someone else's truck in her parking lot. Someone else with the same Auburn University license plate on the front bumper. No. She was right. "I saw your truck. Parked under the tree."

"Hmm." At least he had the good sense to look sheepish. "Interesting. You sure it was mine?"

She arched an eyebrow and waited.

"Okay. You caught me. Although I wish you hadn't." He braced his elbows on the table and leaned closer. "I went home, but I couldn't sleep, wondering if anything was happening. So I figured I might as well not sleep in my truck as not sleep in my house." He swiped at the corner of his mouth with a napkin. "I'm sorry if that made you uncomfortable."

Uncomfortable? Was he kidding? It made her feel…a whole bunch of things she didn't want to feel. She'd been down this road with Josh before, and it ended in a whole lot of tears and gallons of ice cream. Her metabolism was too old for that much fudge ripple. Still, one look at him and she realized trying to lie was impossible. "Actually… it helped me fall asleep."

Grinning, Josh sat back and crossed his arms over his chest. "You're welcome."

"So did staying awake all night give you any new insight?"

"Just more questions. None of it makes any sense." Josh ran a hand across his chin, which testified to the fact he had a four-day weekend and hadn't shaved in at least two days. "What was Wade's big deal about getting into the lobby last night? And what did he mean about protecting more of my soldiers?"

Andrea slid her plate to the side with one finger. There was a slight bruise across her knuckles where she'd made contact with Josh's face just two days ago. It felt like so much longer, in so many ways. "The real question is why he's using his files and my office as a safety net."

"We should have asked him those questions last night."

"I feel dumb for not digging deeper."

"You were too busy reeling over him telling you he skipped alcohol and hit heroin. Maybe the drugs made him crazy."

Andrea chewed on the inside of her lower lip. She'd spent years analyzing Brendan's behavior in retrospect, wondering what she'd missed as her brother dove off the cliff into his addiction. Now she'd missed the same signs with Wade. "I don't know. Any drug can cause erratic behavior, even excessive alcohol. But I don't think he was high yesterday. That seemed more like mental illness, and there's never been a single indicator of that from him before." She sighed. "I don't know. Maybe all of this is taking a toll and I'm just way off my game."

Josh sat up and leaned forward. His hand slid across the table toward hers, then stopped a mere inch away, close enough for her to feel the warmth, to make her wish he'd slip that last little bit. "I'd imagine this kind of pressure would do things to your head."

Andrea nodded and swallowed the fear that had crept up once she'd locked her door last night and truly realized the import of the previous twenty-four hours. "I feel like I'm dancing on the edge. It's not what happened that bothers me, but what could have happened." Her ankle throbbed its agreement, and she tried again to shift the conversation. Her job was to listen to other people's problems. Diving into her own had never been comfortable for her.

Waving her bruised knuckles, she said, "Actually, I think the worst injury of the night was to your cheek." The bruise still mocked her. If someone had told her in high school that she'd be responsible for that kind of mark on his face, she'd have been mortified.

Josh slid his finger along his cheek. "Maybe I'll grow a beard to cover it up." He tipped his head at something over her shoulder. "Maybe I should grow one like that guy back there. That would hide a multitude of imperfections."

Like he had any to hide. Andrea looked over her shoulder to find the man Josh was talking about. A heavyset biker in a leather vest sat by the door. "Yeah, you'd have to work long and hard to grow that beard. It would take longer than a four-day weekend, and you can't have one in your job, anyway."

"Speaking of beards…" Josh wadded up his napkin and threw it on his tray. "I'm out of razor blades. Want to go in the PX with me?"

Andrea dragged her fork through her food again. She wasn't sure what it was, but something about getting razor blades with the man felt…intimate. It was probably a childish thought, but it was there nonetheless. "Go ahead. I want to finish eating."

"Are you sure?"

"Josh—" she looked around the room and back up at him "—there are a million people in here and you'll be right up the hall under the same roof. Nothing's going to happen. And a little bit of alone time where I can breathe without worrying might do me good." She forced herself to take a bite of orange chicken, even though the thought of eating made her gag. She just needed a few minutes to beat down any feelings for Josh that floated to the surface.

He looked as if it was against his better judgment but finally, he stood and hefted his tray. "If you're sure."

"I'm a big girl. I've even been to war. I'll be fine."

"Says the woman in the horror movie right before the creature jumps in and grabs her."

"Really?" Andrea's fork clicked against her plate as she dropped it. "Did you really just make that analogy?"

Holding out both hands, Josh stepped back. "Five minutes. Don't go running off anywhere."

"I promise." Andrea watched him dump his trash and disappear around the corner before slumping in her seat. Honestly. God couldn't possibly think it was cute to bring them together under these circumstances. She didn't want to need Josh, but she did. And that just wasn't funny.

She picked at her orange chicken for a few more minutes, then gave up entirely and drained the rest of her soda. She wasn't sure how long he'd been gone, but it felt like more than five minutes. Maybe she should go find Josh. Except she'd promised she wouldn't go anywhere. Two more minutes, then—

Her next breath caught in her throat as her gaze locked on the man at the door. The one dressed in jeans and a navy blue T-shirt who scanned the food court with purpose. The one with the close-cropped dark hair and an angry bruise along one side of his jaw and up into his cheek.

Three blades? Four blades? Razors with batteries?

Josh ran his thumb along the stinging bruise that striped his cheek and squashed thoughts of Andrea as he considered the selection of razors at the Post Exchange. He wasn't one of those guys who was married to a brand. He just wanted whatever was cheapest. And then he wanted to get back to Andrea.

So much for getting a little bit of distance from her. She refused to leave his thoughts.

A cart clipped him from behind and nearly took his knee out from under him as a giggly voice said, "I just ran right into some guy. I'm blaming you for it."

Josh stepped aside, out of the way of the girl who attempted to talk on her cell phone, maneuver her cart and reach for a pack of soap in one smooth motion that didn't quite work without three hands.

This was why he hated shopping on post when it was payday weekend. Too many people packed in not enough space and paying not enough attention. He grabbed the soap and passed it to the woman, who didn't even acknowledge him as she chattered away.

He bit back a sarcastic comment as he slipped around her cart to the other side of the display, although he did drop a muttered, "You're welcome," as he passed. She didn't even notice. So much for gratitude.

He grabbed the nearest pack of razors with the lowest price and headed for the checkout. He didn't like having Andrea out of his sight for this long. This probably wasn't a mess he should be tangled in, but after what happened with her brother...

His phone vibrated against his hip. Without bothering to look at the screen, he answered and propped the cell between his ear and his shoulder as he dug his wallet out of his back pocket. "Walker here."

There was a pause so long he thought the connection died. "Anybody there?"

"Josh?" The whisper was almost too low to hear in the crowded aisle.

He stopped walking, gripped the phone and straightened. "Andrea?"

"It's me." The low hum of her voice spoke of urgency and more than a little fear.

His pulse drove into overtime. Something wasn't right. Andrea Donovan was not the type of girl to carry on whispered conversations with any man. A woman who could pack a punch like she did and stay sane under pressure like the past couple of days wouldn't play that kind of game. "What's wrong?"

"He's here. In the food court." Behind her voice, the noise of the crowd rose and fell.

"Who? Cameron?" Somehow, he knew that wasn't the answer. She'd jump straight in and confront her own patient, even if he had acted loopy last night. Cameron was such a scrawny kid, he wouldn't scare the fleas off an alley cat.

"The guy. From my office. He just came in."

"Tell me you're right where I left you." Josh dropped the razors and pushed past other soldiers and their families.

"I haven't moved." She drew a deep breath. "He's behind me somewhere and hasn't seen me that I know of. I don't know who he's here looking for, but I'm for sure not about to get up and walk across the room to ask him." She laughed softly. "Even if he's not here about me, we're not exactly going to be BFFs after what I did to his jaw. It's looking pretty nasty from my angle."

"No kidding." A smile actually tipped Josh's lips as he headed for the exit. The girl had even more moxie than he thought if she could crack a joke in a situation like this. "Can you see him?"

There was an even longer pause than the one that started this conversation. The only reason he knew she was still on the line was the hum of the crowd in the food court filtering through the phone. "He just went outside."

Moving with urgency, Josh broke through the crowd heading into the PX. Somehow he knew what she'd do next. "Sit tight." It was futile to say it, but he had to try. He slowed and debated whether to head straight for the parking lot or back up the corridor to Andrea in the food court. "Don't you dare try to follow him. I'll be right there."

"Too late. I'm already out the door. He's got the answers to all of our questions, and I'm not letting him out of my sight. Meet you there." She cut the call before he could say another word.

Pushing through the glass doors to the sidewalk was like diving into a hot tub. The air was almost too thick to breathe. Heat shimmered off the asphalt in waves as Andrea crossed the narrow drop-off lane to the median at the edge of the main lot. She scanned the vehicles from the sidewalk. Not one of the cars moving up the aisles or toward the exit matched the description of the burgundy sedan she'd heard Josh give to the police on Thursday night.

Several people crossed the drop-off lane that separated the building from the larger parking area, and Andrea studied each one as she turned back toward the building. Nobody looked even remotely familiar. A last-ditch search of the tree line on the other side of the parking lot didn't even reveal a suspicious shadow in the woods, let alone sunlight glinting off a rifle barrel like she half-expected.

Andrea fought off the urge to stomp her foot like a two-year-old. There was no way the guy could have vanished like that unless someone waited for him out front. She glanced at the other end of the lane where a Military Police car typically sat. Only a late-model SUV idled there. Of all days for the MPs to skip a patrol…

A figure seemed to materialize from the crowd halfway down the building, waving for her to get back inside. Josh. Even with all that was happening in the moment, his appearance did something to her. Instead of heeding his warning, she deliberately turned back to survey the cars one more time. Something wasn't right. Either she was growing paranoid or she was developing a sixth sense, but even the midday sun seemed to be holding its breath.

The three-chorded chime of her cell phone broke her concentration, and she glanced at the screen, then answered. She knew what the order would be before Josh even uttered it. "Fine," she said, preempting Josh's directive. "I'm heading back inside now. You coming?"

"I'd hoped you were smarter than to follow the guy into the parking lot."

"Well, what do you expect me to do? Let him vaporize into thin air again?" Dragging her hands through her hair, Andrea stepped off the curb to cross the lane between the two sidewalks, studying the front of the building. Could the man have ducked back into the Post Exchange through another door?

Tires squealed. A woman shrieked. Josh yelled something she couldn't decipher as it echoed across the space between them and through her phone at the same time.

Andrea jerked her head up in time to see the small SUV gaining speed as it aimed up the lane toward her.

She barely had time to draw a breath before a force slammed into her, driving her down and back into the grass of the median so hard that her lungs compressed. Her head jerked back and hit the ground, shooting stars across the sky. The blow knocked all of the sound from her world.

It rushed back in an onslaught of squealing tires, shouts and screams.

"Stay with me, Donovan." A deep voice cut through the roar in her head, and she fought to grasp it, to hold on and pull herself out of the chaos.

Brown eyes swam into focus and drew her up to the surface. She sucked in a breath that shuddered its way past her tight throat and exhaled so loud it drowned out all of the noise in her head. "I'm okay." The words were weak, but at least they were audible.

"You're sure?" Josh didn't look convinced.

Before Andrea could answer, an MP broke through the mass of bodies, said something into his radio and knelt on her other side. "Ma'am, are you okay? Can you move?"

For the third time in two days, Andrea heard sirens in the distance, drawing closer, all because of her. She tried to wave off the crush of people around her, crowding her, sucking up all of the oxygen and elevating the already stifling temperature.

"If these people would back up," she muttered, desperate to get a deep breath, "I could stretch out my legs and we'd all know for sure."

The young MP seemed a bit amused at her outburst, but he stood and waved the crowd back as another uniformed policeman arrived to help corral people.

Andrea stretched her limbs and rubbed her lower back. "Did the car hit me?"

"No. That would be me." Josh dropped to the ground beside her, resting a gentle hand on her shoulder to keep her from sitting up. "Wait for the medics to check you out."

That probably wasn't a bad idea, the way her whole

body ached. "Getting tackled by you hurt almost as bad as the car probably would have."

"Sorry." He looked it, too. And shaken up, to boot.

Easing her head from side to side, Andrea felt the tenseness of her neck muscles. This would hurt a whole lot worse tomorrow than it did today. "Did they hit anybody else?"

Josh shook his head and brushed the hair out of Andrea's eyes. "Nobody else was in the crosswalk, and they made a straight line for you. I saw the whole thing. What hurts?"

"I was taken out by a soldier." Andrea grimaced. "What do you think hurts?"

Josh's eyes clouded. "This isn't the time to be cute. You could have been killed."

Killed. The word crawled across Andrea's skin into her ear, where it buzzed, brushing every other sound away. It fogged her vision and sent tremors through her. *Killed.* This time, she couldn't stop the fear from snaking into her nervous system.

"Hey." Josh scooted closer and gently gripped her face between his palms, hovering over her like he meant to protect her from the entire universe. "I'm right here. Look at me. You're okay."

His brown eyes swam into focus inches from hers. She put all of her energy into them, trying to hang on to what seemed like the only solid thing in her life at the moment. *You could have been killed.*

He pressed a kiss to her forehead, then another voice spoke as Josh moved out of her field of vision and a dark-haired woman in a blue uniform appeared. "Thought we were going to lose you there for a second." She snapped latex gloves onto her fingers and picked up Andrea's wrist to check her pulse.

"I'm fine." One more good deep breath cleared the air around her and dissipated the last of the lightheadedness, though her hand still shook in the paramedic's grasp and the buzz in her head grew louder, melding into words. *Killed. You could have been killed.*

SIX

With her blinds closed against the afternoon sun and who knew what else, Andrea's apartment seemed more like a submarine than a home. The light filtered through the blinds, and the air felt oppressive even as the air conditioner fought valiantly against the July heat.

The feeling of suffocation had nothing to do with the atmosphere.

When Josh had retrieved her phone outside the PX, there had been another picture, one of the two of them in the food court, taken from somewhere near the video game store. Whoever was watching knew she'd been there all along. Chances were good they'd never intended to try to run her down but had jumped on the opportunity when she stepped outside.

Andrea stared at her hands as she sat on the navy blue love seat. Deep scratches joined the bruises she'd joked about earlier, and nothing felt funny anymore. She twisted her fingers together and looked up, prepared once again to face off with the detective in front of her. "I can't legally tell you anything about Wade Cameron without a court order. You know that. I'm sorry."

Detective Simmons, a tall, stocky woman in dark trousers and a white shirt, pulled the oversize ottoman away from Andrea's seat and settled onto it.

As she did, Josh sat forward on the couch as though he meant to protect Andrea from whatever hardball the detective might pitch next.

Andrea shot him a grateful look and forced her attention back to the woman in front of her. Josh hadn't needed to stay once he'd driven her home, but there seemed to be some instinct that pushed him to do it, something that told him he had to. Andrea wasn't sure what it was, but now that things were escalating, she was grateful not to be alone with a detective whose bedside manner rivaled Nurse Ratched's.

"Fair enough, Ms. Donovan." Detective Simmons tapped her pen against the notebook she held. "You can't tell me anything about Wade Cameron without a court order. To be honest, I'm not sure there's enough grounds to get one. But you need to be thinking really hard about what you *can* legally tell me. This is looking more and more organized. And less and less like Cameron has anything to do with it." She stood and paced the beige carpet to the window, where she tipped one slat of the blinds with her finger and peered at the parking lot below. "I was prepared to call Thursday night a fluke. And under ordinary circumstances, I'd write yesterday's shooting off as coincidental vandalism. But we have to take into account these pictures you're receiving, and it can't be a coincidence that you saw the same man in the PX and then were nearly run down in the parking lot." Seeming satisfied with her proclamation, she turned away from the window. "And you're one hundred percent certain the guy in the PX was the same guy who attacked you at your clinic?"

"She's certain." Josh's voice was harder than the detective's stare. "I doubt you forget the face of the man who tried to kidnap you."

Andrea's tense neck muscles relaxed. She wasn't alone. His motives were a mystery, but he was here nonetheless, and that was enough. She shot a quick thank-you in his direction then turned to the detective. "I'm sure."

"All right. That leaves me one more question. Why? You tell me why this is happening to you. Let's pretend for a second that Wade Cameron isn't even on the radar here. What else would make somebody do this to a counselor from Columbus, Georgia?"

Drawing her lower lip between her teeth, Andrea stared unseeing at the wall, flipping through images in her mind. Nothing stood out. Finally, she shook her head. "Not a thing. And even if you factor in Specialist Cameron there's still nothing. His stealing drugs from them wouldn't bring them to me, even if he did hide something in his file. If that was all they needed, they wouldn't be so intent on coming after me personally."

That didn't satisfy the detective one bit. In fact, it set a whole new glint in her flat blue eyes. "Nothing at all, huh?" She stalked the room until she stood right in front of Andrea, staring straight down at her. "What exactly are you mixed up in, Ms. Donovan?"

"That's enough." Josh rocketed to his feet like a cannonball. "What is it you're implying?"

Andrea swallowed hard, her mind slow to grasp the implication of the question, but when it did, anger blasted through her. "You think I did something to cause this? What? What could I possibly be involved in?"

Detective Simmons was unruffled by Josh's menacing stature or Andrea's ire. "You tell me. You deal with a lot of recovering drug addicts. Maybe there's a business on the side that keeps them needing your services?"

Andrea shot up from the couch, her nose inches from the detective's. Words sputtered in her mouth before they poured forth in a rush that bordered on volcanic. "How dare you? I have built my life around seeing people find freedom, and I am not about to let you stand here and imply that I've dragged anyone deeper into bondage. You have no idea what drives me, and until you do—" Josh's hand on her shoulder stemmed the words, but swallowing the rest of her tirade did nothing but send the energy out to her extremities. Her fists, balled at her sides, shook.

"Are we done here?" Josh's level voice dosed the situation with much-needed calm. "If we are, ma'am, now might be a good time to leave."

Detective Simmons appeared to consider Josh's suggestion before she tapped her pen against her thigh, then shoved it into her pants pocket. "We're done for now." She pinned a somewhat apologetic look on Andrea. "And I'm sorry, Ms. Donovan. Sometimes we have to push buttons to see what happens."

Words refused to come. Andrea wanted to say she knew the older woman was only doing her job but, as the one on the receiving end of the accusation, she refused to give voice to her thoughts.

The detective merely nodded and passed a thick white business card to Josh, wisely choosing not to direct any more comments to Andrea. "If anything else happens, please call me. I'd like to tell you we have the resources to keep an eye on her apartment, but we don't. Two strikes in less than forty-eight hours make me nervous."

When Josh glanced at her to gauge her reaction, Andrea shrugged and looked away. It didn't matter what happened after the next five minutes. She was two seconds from a meltdown and just wanted everyone to leave so she could fall apart without witnesses.

She struggled for composure as Josh closed the door behind the detective and turned to her. "At least that's over." The words faded out at the end, and he tipped his head as though to see behind her facade. "Andrea?"

She held up both hands. If he showed her one ounce of sympathy, she'd crumble from the pressure. She'd almost been kidnapped, nearly been killed, been accused of the unthinkable... The last thing she wanted was to crack in front of a man like Josh Walker. Even with all that had happened over the last two days, somehow going to pieces in front of him seemed like the worst thing imaginable.

"I'm okay." Even as she spoke the words, the cracks in her demeanor appeared. "Really." The more she tried to talk her way out of it, the more the tears crowded into her throat. "You can—" her hands trembled "—go." Even as she said it, she knew Josh was not the type of guy to comply.

He sighed and walked back to her. "You really shouldn't stuff all of this inside," he said softly.

The quiet words snapped what was left of her control. When one tear broke free and blazed a trail down her cheek, the rest followed like a battalion on the charge.

Before she could stop him, he wrapped her in his arms and pulled her close against a chest stronger than any fortress around her heart. All of her energy leaked out with her tears, and if he hadn't been holding her up, she'd have slumped to the floor, curled into a ball and cried until the world went away.

What had he gotten himself into? When his arms went around her it had been an impulse, but now that she leaned against him it felt like something more. He stood frozen, unable to fill his lungs as she sobbed against his chest. He couldn't remember the last time he'd had his arms around any woman, crying or not. With Andrea, it felt right. Too right.

As the shock wore off and she continued to cry, instinct took over. He stroked her hair and mumbled words meant to comfort, even though it was gibberish to his ears and probably to hers, as well. Either way, it seemed to work. After the initial gale, the storm passed quickly.

When the shaky sobs calmed to deep breaths, Andrea untangled herself from his arms and sank to the oversize ottoman, staring at the floor between her feet. She swiped at her face with the bottom of her T-shirt and mumbled, "I'm sorry."

Sympathy forced him to sit beside her. He wanted to rub her back, make some sort of contact, but none of it seemed appropriate even though she'd just been pressed against him. He shook the image away and instead rested his elbows on his knees. "Don't apologize. You've had a lot going on. A lesser woman would have cracked a week ago, before it ever even happened."

She sniffed. "Thanks."

Silence settled between them, punctuated only by the occasional sniffle from Andrea. Josh wasn't sure what to do next. He couldn't leave her after what had just happened, but he didn't know what to do with his hands. Should he get her a drink? Offer to turn on the TV? If this were a bunch of guys, he'd... Well, none of his buddies would have soaked his shirt with tears. At least he hoped not. He'd have decked them if they tried.

Andrea cleared her throat. "So you've had experience with crying women?"

"Come again?"

"You're pretty good at the soothing thing. Most guys would have plowed over the detective when they raced down the stairs to run away."

He nodded and sat back, stretching his legs in front of him. "Oh, that. I used to have a dog."

For a second, Andrea didn't breathe.

Just as he was wondering if she were about to cry again, her shoulders shook, and she laughed so explosively he jumped. "What?"

"You had a dog?" More tears spilled out, this time with laughter.

Josh winced. Wow. There was no way he could have botched that one any worse. "Not that you're like my dog, but…" Her contagious mirth trumped his embarrassment. "She was afraid of thunderstorms. And the big guns at the range that sound like thunder. And the garbage truck. And pretty much everything else. She needed a lot of comforting."

"What happened to her?"

"Last time I went to Afghanistan, Mom and Dad kept her for me. When I came back, they sort of gently let me know that they'd gotten attached. I think they would have fought me for custody." He grinned, remembering the way his mom had worked her charm on him.

"Oh, my." Andrea sat farther back on the ottoman and swiped at her eyes. "Thanks. I think I feel better now."

"At least I'm good for something." His mood dimmed until it made even the shaded room seem too bright. He'd failed her today and she'd almost gotten killed. Worse, God had given him the opportunity to redeem himself, to finally make atonement, and he'd walked away and left her alone. Would he ever get it right? With a loud exhale, he pressed his palms against his knees and stood.

"What's wrong?" Andrea looked up at him like she was shocked he'd moved.

"I shouldn't have left you alone."

The look on her face defied his attempt to read it. Josh

expected fear, but this was something he couldn't decipher, something that stilled his feet and tugged at his conscience.

"You couldn't have known. Whoever this is was aiming for me whether you were there or not." Andrea's voice was low as she picked at the piping of the ottoman by her knee.

"But I was there. And I nearly let you get yourself killed."

"You're wrong." She shook her head for emphasis and crossed her legs in a yoga pose. "Why do you blame yourself like that?"

What was with the questions? Had she decided she was the strong one and he was the weak one? "Don't." He yanked his hands from his pockets and crossed his arms over his chest. Either she was a really good actress or the innocence on her face was for real. Josh couldn't believe this line of questioning came without purpose. "I see what you're doing."

"What am I doing?"

"Psychoanalyzing me."

Andrea looked confused, then hurt, like he'd accused her of...well, of selling drugs to her patients. "I'm sorry." She barely whispered the words. "It's a habit."

He held up a hand. "Just don't do it again." If she dug too much, he might just tell her the whole truth. Then, when she kicked him out of her life, he'd never be able to protect her.

"I guess I need to focus on someone besides me." Her smile spoke sadness, then she sighed. "It's easier—" Her cell phone trilled three quick notes, and she pulled it from her pocket to glance at the screen. Confusion knotted her eyebrows, and her *hello* sounded cautious, then her face hardened. "Did you forget something, Detective?"

Josh stiffened, ready to snatch the phone from her hand

and give Simmons a chewing out she wouldn't forget anytime soon.

Andrea must have felt his mood change, because she held up a hand and stood, stepping past him across the room to the alcove that served as her dining area. "Where?" She pulled out a chair, then sank into it almost as if her bones melted.

Unable to read her expression, Josh walked toward her, ready to defend or support, whichever she needed.

"Do I need to do anything?" Andrea listened, oblivious to Josh standing feet away. "I'll be there as soon as I can. Thank you." Without looking up, she clicked off the call and dropped the phone to the table with a clatter.

"What's..." Josh wasn't sure how to word the question without sounding like a possessive boyfriend. He had no right to ask her what the call was about. "Everything okay?"

Andrea nodded. "They caught the guy driving the SUV."

Relief allowed Josh his first deep breath since he burst into her office. "Really?"

She twirled her phone on the wooden table like a spinning top. "He blew full tilt through the guard gate on 185 trying to get away. Instead of getting off the highway, he stayed on and got caught just south of the Harris County line. He was in custody before we ever got back to my apartment."

The Harris County line. Not too many miles from here.

"So, if this is one of the guys after Wade, it's over."

Josh nodded, not quite ready to believe it was that easy, especially after Cameron's admissions last night. He'd seen one too many missions that looked like slam dunks, and in the end he and his soldiers had wound up fighting the hardest battles of their lives.

Her face lost some of its humor. “Can I ask you one favor, if you don’t have plans this afternoon?”

Anything. Josh’s head jerked back as though the thought had slapped him. He wasn’t exactly sure why God had orchestrated all of the “coincidences” of the past few days, but he knew it couldn’t be about his feelings for her. That was more than any man could ask.

Across the room, Andrea stood and studied him. “It’s okay if you have plans.”

“No.” He should have said yes, that he’d be busy for the next week, gone on temporary duty, something. Should have extracted himself before he got in deeper. If God wanted him involved, if he was supposed to make good on what he had made bad, then God could just cross their paths again in the future. But his mouth snatched control from his brain. “What do you need?”

“Just...” She wrinkled her nose and tugged at the hem of her blue T-shirt. The way the material stretched, it was obvious the act was a habit. “It’s stupid, really.”

The urge to make everything better for her gripped him and squeezed tight, like a boa constrictor he’d once seen in Panama. “After the week you’ve had, I can’t imagine you making any sort of stupid request.”

Her hands fluttered like butterflies then dropped to her sides. “The guy has a record. They want me to look at a lineup of mug shots and see if I recognize him.”

The words she wasn’t speaking crystallized in the silence. “You want company?”

“Do you mind?”

“No worries.” If all she needed was moral support, he should be able to do that. “And maybe afterward, you’ll let me make you dinner.” Why had he issued such an invitation?

She nodded. “That works. I’ll take Wade’s file and

we'll see if we can figure out what he put in there besides your name, if that's okay by you. I doubt there's anything there, but we'll see if we can't tie everything together." She shouldered her massive purse and shoved the file into it. "And if this is the guy, I'll make dessert to celebrate." Andrea snatched her keys from the ledge by the front door, seeming lighter than she had since Josh first saw her.

Despite the gravity of the situation, Josh was glad he'd said yes to her request. The prospect of an evening with Andrea far outshone any other activity he could imagine.

Still, the warning voice inside his head refused to be silenced. This couldn't end well. At least not for the walls around both of their carefully guarded hearts.

SEVEN

This would not qualify as the brightest idea he'd ever had.

Josh watched as Andrea settled into a canvas deck chair and propped her feet on the rail to stare out at his backyard. Since she'd identified the guy who'd attacked her, she seemed like a different person. She'd chatted away as they left the police station, talking about her parents' current cruise to Alaska. Even her eyes were lighter, nearly crystal green with relief.

He dumped charcoal in the grill and messed around, pretending to light it, but he couldn't focus on the task. His mind kept thwarting all of his best intentions by sending his gaze to Andrea as she sipped sweet tea and studied the trees that bordered his property, a study in peace and contentment.

It took all of his willpower to fight his imagination. Somehow, he was sure a time machine was nearby, one that compressed time and looped it so his unattainable high school dreams materialized in a bizarre twist. He wasn't even sure who he was right now. Everything in him felt like an awkward high school baseball player in an ill-fitting uniform and a dusty cap.

When he'd bothered to think about the future in high school, it had typically been about Major League salaries.

It wasn't until this moment that he realized Andrea had been beside him in every imagined moment. How had he missed that? For someone he had never actually dated, she sure had insinuated herself into his heart.

"Josh?" Andrea's teasing voice pulled him from past dreams. He shook his head. Dreams didn't mean a thing. They could all die in a fiery instant.

"What's up?"

She took a sip of tea and studied him over the rim of the glass, eyes sparking with silent laughter.

Josh's melancholy evaporated. "What's so funny?"

"Just wondering if the meaning of life is written in that charcoal." She rested the glass on her knee and wobbled it back and forth, tea dangerously close to sloshing out with each tilt. Even without looking, she seemed to instinctively know when she had gone far enough and tipped it the other way.

"I'm not sure what you're saying." The sweet, wavy smell of lighter fluid took over his senses. He wasn't sure which was worse, wanting to hold her when she cried or wanting to wrap his arms around her when she laughed.

"You've been staring at it for a good three minutes. Some host you are. Unlit charcoal's more fascinating than your guest."

"Sorry." He knew his face was red. The heat of embarrassment warmed his skin. Reaching for the matches, he pitched one onto the fire and prayed she'd attribute his coloring to the flaming charcoal. "Just thinking about how life is a big circle sometimes."

Something crossed Andrea's face that robbed her expression of its spark, though her mouth still smiled. "Yes, it is."

Josh was certain her thoughts hadn't been anywhere

near his. If they had… Well, if they had, he wouldn't be held responsible for what happened next.

It was her turn to sink into herself. She watched the tea swirl in her glass, a somber look on her face as though she thought it might be possible to read the future in the sweet amber liquid.

Josh couldn't take being this far away any longer. He grabbed his own glass and settled into the chair next to hers, seeking to lighten the mood. "So now you're the one looking for life's secrets?" He nudged his shoulder against hers. "From personal experience, it's not in your ice cubes."

She chuckled. "What made you join the army?" She tried to make it sound light, but something behind the words told him there were reasons for the question.

"Why did you?" he countered, having zero desire to dig into that discussion. That answer had a way of dragging the afternoon into black places they didn't need to go.

Andrea shrugged, then smiled. "No fair interrogating the interrogator."

On the surface, it was a simple question. He could give her the easy answers. He wanted to serve his country. Wanted to stand for something. And while those things would be true, ultimately they wouldn't be the real reason. He owed Andrea the entire truth, or at least as much of it as he could tell without drowning both of them in a past that she shouldn't know and he'd rather forget.

"So what happened? You went to Auburn on a baseball scholarship. Everybody said you'd go pro." When the words left Andrea's mouth, her cheeks pinked.

Josh's lips quirked into a smile. "You remembered? I didn't think you paid me a lick of attention back then."

Her head jerked up and her eyes latched on to his, conveying something he couldn't read. She opened her mouth, closed it, then took a long swallow of tea before she spoke. "I remember lots of things."

"Like?"

"Like I asked you why you joined the army."

Her comeback made Josh smile. "Fine. You have a good memory." He tipped his glass toward her, then turned his attention to the wind in the trees. "I got scouted, had Major League prospects. When I was a junior..." He ran his tongue along his teeth and wondered how much he should say. He'd stick to the basics. The bare, unemotional basics. "I was in a car accident. Wrecked my throwing arm and blew out my knee." He held up his arm to reveal the long scar that ran from his wrist, across his elbow, and halfway up his triceps. "There was no more power behind my throw. And there's not a ball club out there who wants a guy who can't fire the ball from third to first." That night had changed his life and hers forever.

Andrea stared at him with pity in her eyes. He hated pity. Especially when he didn't deserve it from her, when she didn't know the whole story.

"So you're human." The words were tiny, and they didn't speak of pity at all. They spoke more of understanding, and maybe realization. Not at all what he'd expected.

"Everybody's human."

"Yeah, but sometimes we think people are bulletproof."

Josh snorted and swigged his tea. "Yeah? And who thought I was bulletproof?" He glanced at her again, fighting to keep the surprise out of his expression. "You?"

Deep red stained her cheeks. It was crazy that he could see it creep up on her like a forest fire in a dry wood. What could possibly embarrass her that way? Unless... No. That would be too much, the kind of thing that only happened in movies.

Andrea pressed her feet into the deck railing and stretched her legs. "I joined the army a couple of months after I graduated from high school, so probably around the same time as you."

Realization poked him with cold fingers. "That was right after Brendan died." It still hurt to say that name, especially after the last time he saw his best friend. Ironically, his death had jolted Josh into sanity. He hadn't touched alcohol since the night his mother took his hand and told him Brendan was gone.

Josh wanted to throw himself over the deck rail and run until he was too tired to go any farther. The urge to tell Andrea everything was too strong, and it could ruin their friendship. He swallowed the words and opted for something safer. "You're still trying to save him."

For a long moment she didn't move, then she nodded once, slowly, as though the movement might make the past come back to haunt her in the July twilight. "I joined the army because I wanted to finish what he started." She shrugged and pressed her feet harder against the deck rail, bending her sandals at the arch. "And maybe because I was running from the pain. Three months into my first tour, my convoy hit an IED." The tension in her body radiated until Josh felt his own muscles tighten. "I got a concussion, but four of our guys weren't so fortunate." She shrugged as if it were no big deal, but Josh knew better. He'd seen more than one good soldier hollowed into a shell. If she could stand up to that much trauma back to back, Andrea was even stronger than he'd realized.

Without thinking about the ramifications, Josh picked up her hand, pulling her fingers from their white-knuckle grip on the arm of the chair and twining them with his.

Her fingers were cold and limp until he squeezed lightly, then she tightened them around his.

"After I came home and got my head on straight," she continued, "I decided to go to school. I wanted to save the other Brendans in the world." She swallowed and didn't seem to be aware that he was touching her. "Wade's a lot like him. That tall, lanky build and that hair. The minute he walked into my office I noticed it. All of my patients mean something, but with Wade it was almost like God gave me the chance to make up for failing Brendan."

"You didn't fail him." Josh should know. If anyone had failed, it was him.

"I could have done a lot more than I did. I saw him sinking after he came back and took the discharge for PTSD."

Josh slipped out of his chair, careful not to let her fingers inch from his grasp, and crouched beside her. "You were, what? Eighteen? He was a twenty-one-year-old man, capable of his own decisions. There's nothing you could have done."

It finally seemed like she realized he was there. With a sad smile, she looked down at him. "Thank you." There was no emotion, and he knew she couldn't possibly mean the words.

"I try."

She let her eyes scan his for a long time as though deciding something, then forced a smile to her lips. "So, way for me to turn a happy cookout into a downer, huh?"

He grinned, willing to follow her down a new rabbit trail. "Nobody's perfect."

That comment seemed to drive her back into contemplation. "They're not, are they? Maybe that's okay." Andrea let go of his hand and lifted her fingers to the bruise on his cheek, the one she had inflicted. "You look like a prize fighter."

The way her fingers flittered over the tender spot robbed Josh of his voice. All he could do was shrug.

A mischievous grin tipped the corners of her mouth. "So did you win?"

Without bothering to think, he reached up and grasped her fingers. The light in her eyes changed, and he thought she was going to pull away. When she froze, then leaned in slightly, he knew how to answer the question.

Raising up taller on his toes, he let his hand slide beneath the hair at her neck, pulling her closer, his lips hovering against hers. "You tell me."

She inhaled slightly, then his lips were on hers in a pressure he could feel all the way to his toes, in a moment that melted away the last seventeen years and put him in a place where he still believed his dreams could come true. And even though he knew it couldn't last once she found out the truth, he'd take the fantasy for as long as God would let him have it.

At the brush of his lips, Andrea was fifteen again, daydreaming her evenings away in her bedroom, doodling her name and Josh's together in flowing script. Back then, she'd known it would feel like this, that it would consume her if he ever came down off his pedestal and turned his affection to a lowly freshman. She was Cinderella, and the glass slipper fit.

Andrea grasped his biceps and prayed the clock wouldn't strike midnight, that she wouldn't wake up and find out she was still fifteen and dreaming the most lucid dream of her life.

But this was not high school, and it wasn't a dream.

They were both grown-ups, half their lives away from silly crushes. And as long as she had a target on her back, Josh had to be held at a distance. She'd allowed him to dive in too deep already.

Andrea pulled her hands from his arms and sat back, putting distance between them before she could lose herself and instigate their second real-life kiss.

She'd half expected Josh to try to pull her close again, but he let his gaze sweep her face, then backed away. The grill suddenly became particularly interesting to him. He picked up a pair of tongs and poked at the coals, drawing into a shell, lost in thought, as though he could see images in the heating charcoal.

The silence drew out so long it crawled along Andrea's skin and cooled her crazy thoughts. Pulling away was the right thing to do. Not only was she protecting him, but it was clear he was regretting that moment now, no doubt about it. He was probably over there looking for a way to take it all back.

It was for the best. She'd opened her mouth to address their "mistake" when he dropped the tongs onto the deck rail and passed her on the way to the kitchen. "Charcoal's ready. How do you like your steak?"

"However you take yours." It was amazing her voice didn't crack in two. Maybe years of checking her emotions in counseling sessions with patients had unexpected personal benefits.

When the door slipped shut behind him, she dropped her chin to her chest and stared at her knees. After having been attacked three times in as many days, her emotions were too far out of whack for this game. Being alone with her high school dreams was probably one of the biggest mistakes she could have made. The board who had licensed her had to be out of their minds. One of her patients had relapsed into deeper addiction and here she was, the one who should have known infinitely better, doing the same thing. Letting her heart rule her head. Stupid.

The weather stripping around the French door popped to announce Josh's return. Andrea was acutely aware of his presence as he slipped back over to the grill. The steaks sizzled as he dropped them on the grate, and the warm scent of searing meat followed. Even though it ought to be filled with disappointment, her stomach appreciated the distraction.

When Josh settled into his chair, he didn't look at her. Out of the corner of her eye, she watched him lean his head back to stare up at the sky. "I'm sorry," he said, then lifted his head to look at her.

"For what?"

"There's too much you don't know about me for me to drag you into my life." He cleared his throat. "Too much I'm not ready to talk about."

And there it was. Just like she'd known it would be. With the tip of her thumb, she swiped condensation from the side of her glass, too scared to look at him. "No worries. We're both overly emotional after the past few days. Stuff like that would send anybody mucking around in ancient history." The warmth she felt on her lips from his kiss totally betrayed her, but she couldn't let him know that.

The hum of her cell phone vibrated from the deck rail.

Josh nodded slowly, then braced his hands on his chair and heaved himself up. "You're right." He took a deep breath. "You should answer that." He passed her phone to her as he went back to his grill.

Andrea watched him go, then brushed her fingers

across the screen. What little warmth Josh had left with her vanished when she saw what was there. "Josh."

He was by her side before her next breath, and she turned the screen to face him so he could see it.

The picture of them, through the same rifle scope, embracing not five minutes ago. A text followed.

Nowhere is safe until you stop talking.

EIGHT

Josh shoved away from his kitchen table and stretched, rubbing the back of his neck as he yawned. His navy blue T-shirt stretched tight across his abs.

Andrea caught herself looking and turned her gaze back to the contents of the folder spread out on the table in front of her. The police had, once again, come and gone, with the official word that the cell phone being used to taunt her was a prepaid bought with cash in Atlanta. The MAC address of the machine that had pinged her printer was a dead end, as well. Far from being afraid, Andrea was weary with watching over her shoulder.

Fighting the urge to look twice at the man on the other side of the table, she kept unseeing eyes fastened on the page before her. Exhaustion and stress didn't make for a very sound mind, and Andrea wasn't sure she'd be able to control the filter on her mouth if she let her thoughts wander to past feelings. The way he'd backed off after their talk on the deck hadn't cooled that kiss. Neither had that photo.

Oblivious to her thoughts, Josh stood, snagging his mug on his index finger and reaching for hers. "Want a refill?"

"It's getting too late for caffeine."

"You've had four cups and another stalker photo. You really think one more cup is going to tip the scale?"

Andrea bit back a smile as she pulled a piece of paper from the scattered stack in front of her and held it up. The edges fluttered as though a breeze blew through the room, betraying her shaking fingers. "Does it look like I need more stimulants?"

"Water it is. No wonder you left the army. You couldn't keep up with the caffeine intake."

"My discharge papers indicate failure to raise my blood pressure to unsafe levels." Light conversation felt so much better than drugs and threats. She wanted to hug him for playing along.

Josh disappeared behind her as she bent her head over the pages. Her focus vanished as she listened to him refill the coffeepot. Just knowing he was there did something to her heart rate that she couldn't blame on caffeine. Sleep had to come soon. Otherwise, she'd spill out every daydream she'd ever had about him.

The thud of glass on wood raised her head. "Thanks."

"Sure thing." He settled into his chair, the remains of the last pot of coffee nearly spilling over as he took a cautious sip. "So…" He set down his mug and motioned toward the papers he'd read. "I've got nothin'."

She agreed. "There's nothing in my files but notes about sessions. To anyone but me, these are worthless."

"Talk to me about Cameron." Josh slid his coffee mug back and forth between his hands, absorbed in the motion. "Maybe hearing it out loud will help."

It seemed like a waste of time, but what else did they have? Andrea sat back and tilted her head from side to side, stretching too-tight neck muscles. "To be honest, he was a textbook case." She looked up to find Josh studying her with an unreadable look. It took a minute for her flustered mind to draw back to the conversation. "Terrible childhood. Dad drank. Mom did drugs. Wade was taken out of the home when he was in first grade. He bounced around in the foster system until he joined the army."

"Where are his parents?"

"Dad was killed in a car accident. Mom is in prison in Nevada. He tried to see her before he deployed but she refused. She blames him for the family being torn apart."

Josh sniffed and set his coffee cup on the table so hard the dark liquid sloshed over the edge. "Spoken like a true addict. It's everyone else's fault." He swiped at the dark drops on the wood tabletop. "At least Wade learned to take responsibility for his actions. I've never once heard that kid blame anyone else for his troubles."

"Until last night." The voice that squeaked from Andrea's throat was meek. Stealing drugs was stupid, but it didn't cut Andrea like his relapse did.

Josh drummed his finger against the edge of the table. The tapping continued until Andrea wanted to slap her hand down over his, but just when she was about to give in to the urge, he stopped. "Maybe we're coming at this from the wrong direction."

"Meaning?"

"He said he put something in, not that he said something to you. Besides, I think you'd remember Cameron saying, 'Hey, Doc, I stole drugs from some guys and here are their names.'"

"The bad guys don't know that. I'm sure they think he's done just that and I hold the proof. And him putting something in a file wouldn't have them pushing me to close my doors."

"Okay, how about this." He sat up like he'd suddenly thought of the answer. "Who has access to your files?"

"Just me. And Grace. Even though we have release

forms like the one Wade signed for you, I've never had anyone ask." She slid the file closer and shut it to look at the outside, then flipped it open again, the attached patient data sheets flopping against the cover. "It's a pretty simple system. Grace keys the patient data into the computer and passes everything back to me. Unless there's a change, it never—" Andrea stopped, eyes narrowing as she stared at the pages attached to the folder.

"What?"

"We're looking at this all wrong." She flattened her palm against Wade's handwriting on the patient information page, which was clipped securely into the front of the folder. "You're right. He said it was something he did."

Eyebrow arched, Josh leaned closer.

"We thought it was weird he changed the forms so you could see his file." She flipped sheets until she found the one she was looking for.

Josh got up and came around the table, slipping into the seat next to hers.

With effort, she focused on the page and not on his arm brushing hers. "He crossed out his foster father's name and wrote yours. Why didn't Grace give him a clean sheet to fill out? Based on the fact he scratched this out and wrote your name in, she handed him the entire folder." She reached for her phone, which lay beneath a stack of session notes. "I'm calling her. Maybe she remembers—"

"Andrea." Josh pressed her hand against the table. "It's after two. Grace is on vacation and would probably appreciate it if you waited a few hours to make that call."

Heat raced up her arm. For the smallest moment, she let herself enjoy the contact, then slipped her hand from beneath his. "Not quite thinking clearly."

Josh didn't respond for a second, then reached over and slid the folder closer. He flipped through each sheet, mumbling. "Name, address, medical history… My guess is your hulking friend is scared you know something you don't."

"Well, leave no stone unturned." Andrea popped the metal brackets and slipped the papers free. "You take the top three and I'll take…" The thought died as she caught sight of scrawled words between the brackets, where the sheets had been clamped to the folder. "Found it."

Josh laid an arm across the back of her chair and leaned near to read over her shoulder.

She swallowed hard against the closeness and read the scrawled words out loud. "Third wall locker from showers. Bottom panel loose. Don't talk. Office bugs." She stiffened her neck to avoid meeting Josh's gaze way too close to hers. "He left a maintenance request in his file?"

Josh took the folder from her. "That kid is a genius."

"What?" Andrea knew she was tired, but now she felt like she was having a riddle-filled conversation with the Cheshire Cat. Sure enough, a slow smile spread across Josh's face.

"He's smarter than we've been giving him credit for." Josh slipped his arm from her chair and paced to the window, staring out into the darkness. "Nobody's using those wall lockers in the unit. He's just blessed we haven't ripped them out since he wrote this. Whatever is going on, this is his insurance."

Light dawned, and Andrea had to admit Josh was right. She'd always known Wade was a smart kid, but the genius label might just work. "He changed his file because he knew you'd eventually see it. You're one of the only people he knows who'd understand what it meant."

"Yep." Josh turned around to lean against the wall and crossed his arms over his chest.

"But why not just tell you? And why not tell you last night?"

"If anything happened to him, he knew somebody would look into his file and call me. My guess is he didn't know he was in trouble until he got to your place, and then it was too late to tell me. He just had to hope his plan worked." He scratched the darkening stubble on his chin. "None of this explains why he acted like he did last night. He didn't mention any of it, then bolted when we asked him. He could have said it while we were sitting there with no one to hear or see. He's not bipolar or something, is he?"

Andrea arched an eyebrow. "First off, bipolar wouldn't make you forget you wanted to tell your first sergeant something. Second, he's never displayed any mental illness. Outside of addiction, he's as healthy as he can be."

"So why was he acting like that last night?"

"Stress can do crazy things to the mind." Andrea turned in her seat to look at Josh. "Maybe he's manifesting a panic disorder. Especially with him talking about bugs in your office."

"*My* office? There are no bugs in my office."

"Okay..."

"They're in yours."

This was ridiculous. Clearly, the loopiness of the late hour had laid claim to Josh's sanity. "Josh, there's no reason for him to be worried about—" The hard expression he directed at her slashed through the thought. "No." She gripped the edge of the table, nausea roiling in her gut. Somebody had been listening to her sessions, to her phone calls, to her patients...and for who knew how long. Even with all that had already happened, this far surpassed her worst nightmares. This was so much more personal, so much more intrusive. “They’ve been listening? And that’s why he wanted to get out of my office so badly last night?”

“Based on Cameron’s behavior, it’s probably more than listening.” Josh slipped into the chair beside hers and pressed his hands onto the table, studying his fingers. “He kept saying they knew everything.”

Andrea’s eyes slipped shut. Too much stimuli assaulted her at once. “Explain.”

“If it was just a listening device, he would have risked writing what he wanted to say. He was afraid somebody could not only hear us, but see us, and he didn’t want to risk anyone knowing his secrets.”

The feeling of being exposed sent spidery tingles running up her arms, like invisible gazes brushing her skin even as she sat in Josh’s dining room. “How did they get access to my office?”

“Have you had any work done lately?”

“None that… Yes. A couple of weeks ago, we switched to cable internet. Not too long after, a couple of guys showed up and said the initial installation crew was from a new subcontractor and they needed to verify the work.”

“That’s it, then.”

“And that’s when they got access to my printer, too.” Andrea looked away, trying to hide her fear. “But why? Wade wasn’t even seeing me at that point.”

“I have no idea.”

“This all feels like a puzzle that’s missing pieces.”

“Well, I know where one of those pieces is.” Josh shoved the chair from the table and snatched his keys from the bar that edged the dining area. “We’ve got a wall locker to check out.”

NINE

Josh had been at the building that housed his infantry unit at all hours of the day and night, but his workplace had never felt shadowy and dark the way it did in the predawn with Andrea beside him. He knew the place better than his own house, but things felt different tonight. He should have taken her home and come alone instead of exposing her to possible danger. As he suspected, with another picture sitting on Andrea's phone, the guys in the Muscogee County Jail weren't the only ones involved. What if someone else had discovered Wade Cameron's hiding place? The chances that someone would randomly get the message at the same time as they did were incredible, but he'd seen crazier coincidences enough times to know that anything was possible.

Josh tried not to telegraph his concern to Andrea as he switched off the truck and scanned the shadows at the edges of the buildings, where streetlights didn't quite cut the thick darkness. "Ready?"

Andrea didn't look ready. It wouldn't surprise him if she had the ability to read his mind and knew exactly where his concerns lay. He could see her eyes in the dim light. She took in everything. Finally, she took a deep breath, seemed to remember he was there and to draw some sense of peace from his presence. "Let's rock and roll."

The door locks popped open, and they climbed out and met at the front of the truck. She lifted a hand toward him, then dropped it to her side. "Are you sure nobody's watching us?"

That possibility had circled his head more than once and had finally been dismissed. "Whoever this is has proven they know how to get on post, but nobody followed us out here, not unless they were driving without head-lights. Around here, that's a good way to hit an armadillo."

"Or a wild boar." She relaxed the slightest bit. "What do you think he's hidden in there?"

"Who knows?" Josh dropped his cell into the cargo pocket of his shorts and jingled the keys in his hand. "He said he hid their drugs. Depending on the amount, they could be in there." His feet slid to a halt as he stopped walking and stared at the building. "Although that would be exceptionally stupid."

"In an unused wall locker, how would anybody know who they belonged to or how long they'd been there? I'd say it's pretty smart."

Josh reached for her elbow and guided her forward, still surveilling the area. Nothing moved outside of a slight breeze in the tops of the trees, though the air in the park-ing lot was heavy and still. "This is true, but it would also invite a one hundred percent drug test for the entire battalion. Since there's no way to know if or when they'd be found, it's asking for trouble if somebody gets caught in that test and they're using. Anybody who came up hot would be out for blood."

"Then again, maybe he wants anybody using to get caught and forced into getting help."

"Spoken like a true head doctor." Josh let his hand slide

down her arm but stopped just short of taking her hand. Until he told her the truth, she was off-limits in nearly every way. His job was to protect her, to make amends for what he'd already made wrong in her family. Josh let go of her arm and placed his palm against her back, desperate to shield her even if he couldn't have her.

"Occupational hazard. Everyone gets psychoanalyzed."

"Going to take another crack at figuring me out?" Josh kept his tone light, but it mattered what she thought about him and how well she could see through the facade he'd erected so long ago.

They stopped at the entrance to the company and she turned to face him, leaning her shoulder on the doorjamb. "Do you really want me to answer that? Here? Now?"

"You think I can't handle it?" The lock stuck as he turned the key and the door gave resistance as he pushed it open. He made one last survey of the parking lot as he ushered her inside. "I'm a company first sergeant in an infantry unit. I pass down the info guys don't want to hear and hold them to the standards they don't always want to be held to. There's nothing you can say as bad as what some of them have spouted behind my back. Or as bad as some of their wives have screamed in my face."

"I can imagine." Her chuckle sounded forced, echoing off the walls as she stepped into the building ahead of him. "I can remember how I felt about some of my first sergeants. Now that I'm older, the things they were doing back then make more sense."

"Does this mean I'll get about a thousand apology letters from these guys in a decade or so?"

"Only if those wild hogs around here sprout wings. But I'll guarantee you they'll never forget you. Just like you've never forgotten any of your old first sergeants.

You knew who cared and who didn't, even if you didn't always want to admit it, right?"

"Spot on." Inside, he didn't flip on the lights. Instead, he let the darkness settle around them as the door thudded shut. "And now that you've nailed that one, you can tell me what your psychoanalysis of this old first sergeant is." His voice dropped huskier than he meant, but it was too late to take the words back.

The change in Andrea's breathing was audible in the darkness. "I don't think anything."

He caught her hand. As his eyes adjusted, Josh could make out the faint outline of her. "No. You don't have to censor yourself." Knowing how Andrea saw him mattered more than anything Wade Cameron could have hidden in the base of a busted wall locker.

"Okay." She pulled in a deep breath. "You're hiding something."

"I don't know what you're talking about."

"You do."

The false anonymity of the dark room loosened his inhibitions and made him want to spill everything. In spite of the sense of danger that refused to be shaken, there was safety here between them, safety he wasn't sure he wanted to shatter by telling her about the night her brother died. Spilling his guts onto the floor could be more dangerous than anything Andrea had faced in the past couple of days.

That feeling made him doubly sure he shouldn't have kissed her earlier. It had been monumentally unfair to her. The look on her face if she found out who he really was would be more than he could bear. "Sorry, Doc. You missed that one completely." He dropped her hand in a vain effort to break the connection that grew stronger every second.

"I don't know what it is," she whispered, "but there's

more to the story than you're telling." Her fingers brushed the scar on his arm, tightening his stomach. "You weren't alone in that car wreck."

Adrenaline jolted his heart out of rhythm. "What makes you say that?"

"The things you don't say when you talk about the wreck. This sort of overinflated protector streak you have. Who was she?"

The air hung heavy with an intimacy he'd never felt before. Half of him wanted to reach out and pull her to him, to spill everything and hold on tight to what existed here and now so the bad couldn't beat its way in. The other half wanted to shove her aside and run until no one ever found him again. When her fingers tightened on his biceps, his mouth made the choice to tell her about the accident, even if he still buried everything that happened before it. "Blind date. Lauren. I barely even knew her." Even now, he couldn't recall her face, which only amped the wattage of his guilt.

"Was the wreck your fault?" She swallowed so hard he could hear it. "Were you drinking?"

The urge to smile at her assumption was trumped by how close to the truth the question was. "Not that night. Fortunately. And never again after." Not after what he'd seen happen to Brendan that same night.

Josh leaned a shoulder against the door, hoping it was strong enough to hold up the weight of his mistakes. "I lost control of my SUV when a tire blew and it rolled." His voice sounded too big for the small space between them.

Andrea's touch trailed down his arm, raising goose bumps in its wake. She gripped his fingers, pulling them from the door handle and lacing them with her own. He hadn't realized he was gripping so tightly until she touched him.

"Like an idiot, I wasn't wearing a seat belt and got thrown from the vehicle. Oddly enough, that's probably what saved my life." He swallowed an all-too familiar nausea.

"She died." There was a knowing, like she'd heard the story before and was hoping the ending would change.

The pity didn't anger him as it had from so many others in the past. From Andrea, it was sincere, almost like she wished she could make the outcome different. "Vehicle caught fire. I tried to get to her, but…" The memory shot phantom pain through his scarred arm. "I was too far away. The injuries to my knee and arm made me too slow." He dragged his sight back from the nightmare of the past to the darkened silhouette of the woman in front of him. "I tried. And I couldn't. The pain took me out. When I came around, the EMTs were there and it was over. Everybody told me she died before the fire, but that never stopped the nightmares."

Andrea squeezed his hand in a way that made him want to connect. The urge to close the distance between them and kiss her, to feel alive and grounded in a completely different kind of moment nearly overwhelmed him.

"Nightmares aren't uncommon after trauma."

The matter-of-fact statement dashed cold reality all over his emotions. Her interest in him was strictly clinical, and she was a threat to his sanity, ripping open boxes of memories he'd sealed shut. He had to find a switch and throw light between them. Fast.

Josh yanked his hand from hers and backed away. "Know what? I never should have said anything."

"Josh…"

"Forget it." His fingers brushed the plate below the switch. "It's better if—"

The sound of a door opening somewhere in the building cut off the rest of his words.

Beside him, Andrea gasped.

He grabbed her wrist, grateful he hadn't given away their position by flipping a light switch. Much longer and he'd have exposed them to whoever lurked nearby. Intuition had told him the danger wasn't over, yet he'd dropped every guard he had. Now Andrea might pay the price.

Without a word, he pulled her through the small room lined with wall lockers until they reached the bathroom. The sickly sweet smell of old shampoo and sweaty gym clothes weighed heavily in the stale air. Amazing it had never seemed so strong before, but in the dark, looking for a position from which he could protect Andrea, it was almost more than his stomach could handle.

For the first time ever, Josh was grateful for every minute he'd spent in this building. By instinct, he knew exactly where to turn. Within seconds, they stood in the far corner of the room, away from the door. The only flaw with the plan was there was no way out if someone found them.

He gripped Andrea's shoulders as though he could look her in the eye if he tried hard enough in the blackness. "Don't move."

"How'd they find us?" Far from the frightened utterance he'd expected to hear, her voice was level and calm.

"I don't know." He wanted to tell her she shouldn't worry, that he'd protect her, but it felt too much like lying. Instead, he pressed his lips to her forehead and whispered, "Wait here." He squeezed her shoulders one more time then inched toward the door, unarmed, listening to footsteps that drew closer with each breath.

Numb. That's all she was. It felt like she was watching herself on a movie screen instead of existing in this moment. Disassociation could happen under stress, but

Andrea had never known it to this degree. Terror ought to have her plastered to the floor, but all she could muster was a cold resignation that scared her even more. They were backed into a corner. If the rest of her life was going to be spent hiding in shadows, it might be better to step out now and let the insanity end tonight. Stark defeat had never been part of her makeup, but she couldn't handle being stalked at every move, couldn't live with the uncertainty of the whole situation. Whatever Wade had gotten into, it was bigger than she'd imagined.

From across the room, she could hear Josh breathe. Even though his shape was difficult to discern, it was impossible to ignore his presence. This wasn't his fight, yet there he stood, on the front lines, willing to protect her to the end.

The idea caught her in the chest and stole her next breath. He'd been there from the first moment she'd stepped into this nightmare, walking beside her, never once hesitating to come to her defense. There wasn't a thing she could offer him in return, not one reason for his involvement. After the story he'd just told her, it was beyond belief he hadn't run fast in the other direction when faced with her mounting problems. Andrea blinked long and slow, then opened her eyes again, allowing herself to surrender to someone else's help for the first time in her memory. *God, I don't know why he's here...but thank You.*

Voices drifted to her tiny corner, though her ears buzzed too much from a surge of adrenaline to make out the words.

Josh chuckled, the sound as out of place as a lake in the desert. "Stay here," he whispered as he stepped closer. "Whatever you do, don't come out."

When he left the room, he took all of the air with him. Andrea pressed her back against the cool wall, trying to shrink as small as possible. What was he doing? He couldn't confront those guys head-on and unarmed.

She blinked against light that suddenly flooded in from the hallway.

"This is First Sergeant Walker." Josh's commanding voice barged into the room and pounded in her ears.

Was he crazy? The bad guys weren't going to care who he was. Shock fused her spine to the cinder block wall.

Laughter came into the room next, followed by more voices. Even though Andrea figured they were both insane, the sound of Josh's shared laughter washed over her and ebbed the tide of terror. Things were going to be okay.

This time.

Josh reappeared, silhouetted in the doorway. She'd missed it before, how broad his shoulders were, how his waist narrowed at his hips and cut a figure that spoke of strength and assurance.

Hang her independence. She needed him. For the first time in as long as she could remember, she wanted to climb into someone's arms and let them shield her from the rest of the world. Instead, Andrea pulled in a long breath and noticed the smell of old locker room for the first time. Her nose wrinkled. "It stinks in here."

"Well, yeah." Josh crossed his arms and leaned a shoulder against the doorway. "Dozens of guys in their sweaty physical training uniforms are in and out of here every day. You ought to figure it wouldn't smell like a European spa."

Andrea fought to get her feet on level ground. She'd been jerked from laughter to danger to whatever now surged between them all in the span of ten minutes. It was like someone had determined to drop all of life's most stressful moments onto her in one evening, just to see how she'd react. "I'm guessing we're okay?"

"Yep. Someone saw us come in the building and called staff duty. They came over to make sure nothing hinky was going on." He looked away from her at something up the hall. "Just about the last thing I need is them to find me hiding out in a dark bathroom with a beautiful woman. There's no telling what kind of tales would fly around this place."

Beautiful woman. The words settled on her shoulders like a blanket. After the way he'd rejected her at his house and pulled away from her a few moments ago, surely he didn't mean that the way it sounded.

Josh straightened and crooked a finger at her. "All right, Tonto. We've got a wall locker to tear apart."

So that was it. One more whiplash. If this kept up, Andrea would either be in a neck brace or dead by the time the sun rose.

Well, now he'd done it. His mouth had gotten away from him for sure this time. First he'd told her everything he'd never said to another person, then he'd made it infinitely worse. The instant the word *beautiful* left his mouth it smacked her in the face. Josh had seen the way her eyes clouded and her brows drew together and knew it was the wrong thing to say. It was probably not the word she wanted to hear from a man who'd just confessed to killing a woman he'd barely known.

The fact he was responsible for that death and that he still hadn't told her the whole story pierced his heart with fresh pain. He had to prove he could be counted on in the clinch, and Andrea was definitely in the grip of something that could cost her her life. The last thing he needed was to let his emotions trip him up. No matter who she was, no matter that she truly was the most beautiful woman he'd ever known, that feeling had to die.

But he couldn't stop noticing her.

The way she trailed behind him up the hall lined with metal lockers reminded him of some of the kids he'd interacted with overseas. They were always hesitant to trust at first, wanting to get close but unsure if the American with candy and a gun was safe. That was Andrea right now, debating her safety. As she should.

Josh stopped in front of the indicated bank of wall lockers, nearly passing them in his self-recrimination.

Andrea stumbled and rested a hand on his back to stop herself from falling. So she'd been closer than he'd thought. Man, did she ever throw his radar off.

Josh pretended her touch didn't do a thing to him and studied the third locker from the showers, as Cameron had indicated. It looked like any one of the identical lockers lined up beside it. He squatted to rest on his heels and rapped the metal with his knuckles, wary of what it might contain. It hadn't been an immediate concern before, but what if the thing were rigged? It could go off in both of their faces. "Maybe we should call the MPs."

She sniffed and knelt beside him. "Why? So they can accuse me of more crimes just to gauge my reaction?"

"Since when did you become such a cynic?"

"Since it was suggested I'm dealing drugs to a recovering addict." She puffed her cheeks and exhaled slowly, wrapping her arms around her stomach. "I know. They have to do their job, but..." Her sigh brushed his neck. "That one cut."

As much as Josh wanted to reach over and pull her close, he coached his muscles against the impulse. God had a strange sense of humor, putting him in this position.

"You're wondering if that thing's going to blow when you open it, aren't you?" Her voice shook slightly.

He nodded and tried to ignore her proximity. "Impressive mind reading. They teach you that in school?"

"Woman's intuition." Andrea pressed her hands to her thighs and stood, her knees popping as she did. "Tell you what..." Without hesitation, she snapped the latch and yanked the locker open without so much as a flinch.

Josh would never confess he blinked.

But nothing happened. He found himself staring at the scuffed floor of a completely empty wall locker.

"He said the bottom panel's loose." Andrea's voice rained down from where she stood above him. "Get a move on that one, soldier."

Josh flipped her a mock salute. "That panel could be what's rigged, you know."

"Man up, son. We all gotta go sometime."

She was cracking jokes at a time like this. Then again, she'd done it before. Must be where she hid when she was scared, behind that twinkle in her eye. Weirdest stress reaction he'd ever seen.

"I notice you're up there and I'm down here." He stretched his arms forward, laced his fingers and cracked his knuckles. "Okay. I'm goin' in."

No answer met his jest.

Josh ran his hand along the sides of the panel, wishing he'd brought a screwdriver to pop the piece, but he found a notch near a bend in the back corner, just large enough to slip his finger into. "Here goes nothin'." He hooked his finger under the base of the metal and pulled.

Andrea drew back with a shudder. How many times could she wait to die in one day? When no explosion blasted through the room, she cracked one eye open and looked down.

Josh grinned up at her. "Looks like we're still here."

Her cheeks burned. Weakness was not something she liked to show. "Yep." She squatted beside Josh as he lifted the panel out of the way.

Empty.

Dust and cobwebs clung to the corners of the metal and lay on the floor underneath, but no clue greeted them.

Dropping all the way back to sit on the floor, Andrea stared into the empty wall locker. "That's that." She dragged her hair over her shoulder and let the ends sift through her fingers. "Any more brilliant ideas?"

Disappointment bit at the base of her neck. She didn't know what she'd hoped to find there—the name of the guy who'd attacked her, maybe?—but sheer emptiness sure didn't fit anything she'd expected.

Josh pressed two opposite corners of the locker base against his palms and set it spinning in his hands. "We could pull the bottoms off this whole row. Maybe he counted wrong. He's a bright kid, though. My guess is he can count to three."

Andrea chuckled and watched Josh flip the metal over and over. When she saw a smudge of red on the underside of the plate, she grabbed Josh's arm.

He froze and looked over his shoulder like a knife-wielding maniac had crept up on them.

Without explanation, Andrea snatched the metal from his hands and flipped it over to the underside. There, in red marker, the notation *5977 WhVi D4* ran from corner to corner.

Josh whistled low. "Think it's Cameron's?"

Andrea held the flat metal at eye level and studied it in the light. "It's not old. The ink's not dirty like some of the metal around it. It's actually written over some of the dust. Even if it's not his, it's recent. Why would any of your other guys be writing on the bottom of this particular locker? Or any locker, for that matter?"

"Why do nineteen-year-olds do anything?" Josh slipped the piece from her hands. "Make any sense to you?"

"None. How about you? Is it some kind of secret code they're teaching in basic training now?"

Josh nodded slowly and angled the metal from one side to the other as he studied it. "Yeah." His voice deepened in concentration. "It's in a course on how to hide a stolen drug stash from the dudes who want it back."

When Andrea chuckled, Josh dropped the metal onto his lap and sat back, bracing his hands on the floor behind him. "Question is, now that we have it, what do we do with it?" The sentence ended on the stretch of a yawn.

Andrea followed suit. "Use it as a pillow?"

He picked the locker bottom up from his lap and thunked it against the floor. "I've slept on worse. But get serious. You're getting the oh-dark-thirty sleepless and loopy brain."

"Probably." Andrea folded her knees to sit cross-legged facing him. "I've got enough on my plate trying to protect that file. You want to hold on to the hunk of metal?"

"So they can ransack my house later? No." He tilted his head to stare at the ceiling.

Andrea studied his profile. It was no wonder he'd stepped into the role of leader so well in the army and had advanced as far as he had. He had that "look" about him, the kind that commanded authority. Kingdoms were built on jawlines like that, she was sure of it.

Would she never learn? When he pulled his head to one side and then the other to stretch his neck, she dropped her gaze to her hands knit together in her lap. She'd done enough staring at him in high school. Considering his nonchalance over their earlier kiss, it sure wouldn't do to get caught engaging in that particular pastime now.

Josh rolled his shoulders and sat up, dusting off his hands. "I say we leave it where we found it."

Andrea arched an eyebrow. "Seriously?"

"Think about it. It's been safe here all along. The guys on twenty-four-hour duty will know if anybody comes in. Look how quick they came looking for us. And without the file to know there's something interesting about this wall locker, it's not an obvious guess. Cameron's counseling history was scattered all over my kitchen before we figured it out. If you're really worried about someone finding it in the file, a little Sharpie works wonders on things you want to hide."

"We can't destroy evidence."

He twisted his lips together. "Yeah. Hadn't thought of that. Maybe we'll dump the file under here, too. You can't find the hiding place if you hide the clue to the hiding place in the—" his eyebrows drew together "—hiding place."

"Now who's got oh-dark-thirty brain?"

He raised his hand like a schoolboy. For a second, Andrea caught sight of the young man she'd known so long ago. She turned her focus to the filthy floor under the locker and nodded. "I'll second the motion. Leave the piece here. And when we figure out if it's important, we'll pass it along to the police. Right now, I'm afraid of what they'll think of me if I show up with one more piece of hidden evidence." She dug into her pocket and pulled out her cell phone.

Catching her intention, Josh held the panel still while she snapped pictures and texted them to him, as well.

Josh sat up and slipped the panel into the locker. With a sharp, metallic *pop,* the bottom snapped into place and Josh stood, wiping his hands on the legs of his shorts.

When he seemed satisfied, he held a hand out to Andrea. "Well, m'lady, we should get you home before you turn into a pumpkin."

She grasped his hand and wished the feeling didn't run straight to her heart.

Too late. Cinderella broke her glass slipper hours ago.

TEN

Josh jammed the key into the ignition of his pickup and stared across the parking lot at the tiny church nestled at the edge of the trees. It was a few minutes after noon and heat waves already shimmered from the asphalt to mute the edges of the white clapboard building. He could be downtown at his church right now, where he blended into the megacrowd, but no, somehow in the faded light of dawn, when she'd asked him to come to her church with her, he'd said yes.

Now he sat in the parking lot, waiting for Andrea to finish a "brief" meeting of the church's education council, and wondered why he was here.

A knot of parishioners drifted down the steep brick steps. The women shrugged out of sweaters as they hit the heavy July humidity. The church had AC and it had been cranking. The facilities, he thought, were certainly not as ancient as the structure.

"Ancient." The word ricocheted like a bullet through the truck as he spat it, shocked that it had been out loud. Their late-night scavenger hunt had occupied most of his energy, but the minute circumstances had slowed down enough to allow his thoughts to wander, frustration reared its head. After that kiss, he'd been seconds from telling Andrea what he'd really thought about her in high school, how that tongue-tied state still seemed to plague him when he was in her presence. Yeah, he'd been the one to back off, to realize nothing could happen with his secret between them. Then she'd written the whole thing off as *ancient history*. It had been the jolt he needed. It was their past, and it needed to stay there. He was a confirmed bachelor for a reason, and he sure didn't deserve to love someone like Andrea, not with the responsibility for Brendan resting squarely on his shoulders.

So why was he here? Because he was a sucker for a pretty face.

Josh ran a hand across his chin and chuckled. That's it. Next time he couldn't sleep, he had to avoid any channel showing film noir classics. He couldn't spend the rest of the day sounding like Humphrey Bogart. He'd already dumped off what was left of his common sense by coming here with her.

And agreeing to lunch.

He shook his head and exhaled loudly. How long could he lie to himself and say it was only because God wanted him to protect her, to make up for letting her brother die? He was still as selfish as he was all those years ago. Truth was, it was about him. All of it.

The parking lot was nearly empty and Josh had switched on the air-conditioning when Andrea appeared at the door to the church. She caught his eye and waved him inside.

Annoyed with himself for hanging around, Josh cut the ignition and slid out of the truck, pocketing the key ring as he strode across the nearly molten asphalt toward the church. He really should say something had come up and he couldn't make lunch. But the closer he got to her, standing in the doorway in white capris and some sort of loose purple shirt, the less he wanted to walk the other way. It mattered less what she thought of him and more that he could spend time with her.

Andrea had stayed up half the night replaying that kiss and kicking herself for diving into it. And for asking him to take her to church today. Which was worse: his thinking she was desperate for his attention or his thinking she was terrified to go along with her normal routine? Either way, she wore humiliation like a veil, and she'd only magnified it last night by telling him her high school secrets, which he kicked to the side and ignored.

Sitting in the pew beside him had been awkward, to say the least. She was already stiff from his linebacker tackle at the PX yesterday, and her muscles jolted each time his elbow brushed hers. The whole "couple in church" thing was too intimate and raised too many eyebrows around her tiny congregation. It seemed she'd never learn to think her impulses through.

When the short "when should we meet to plan the fall Sunday School rally" discussion turned into a full-on planning session, Andrea had called Josh in to let him know it could be a while. Far from leaving the way she'd expected him to, he'd settled in the pew beside her and sat listening as if he belonged there, although a storm brewed behind his eyes.

She'd never hear the end of it from Berta Summers, the church matriarch who'd been trying to marry her off for her entire ten-year stint in this congregation. Andrea glanced around at the dozen people scattered about the room. Truth be told, she'd never hear the end of it from any of them.

A sigh slipped out. Boy, would she hate to have to change churches now, but it might be the only way to avoid a game of twenty questions every time she stepped through the door or ran into one of them at the Winn-Dixie for the next month.

Josh leaned closer, his shoulder brushing hers. Andrea thought she would leap out of her skin and grip the ceiling. "You okay?"

The motion and the quiet words drew the attention of half of the Sunday School board.

Yep. She'd never hear the end of it.

Andrea nodded and waited for curious eyes to drift away. "Starving." It wasn't a lie. It just wasn't the answer to the question he'd asked.

Josh nodded and rubbed his hand across his stomach, pressing his shirt over abs too flat to be real.

Andrea stifled a groan and turned her attention back to Giles Martin at the front of the church. She hadn't needed to see that. Not now, when her imagination was doing a fine job of its own. Time had been way too good to Josh Walker. Better than it had been to her.

Josh's elbow found her ribs and begged for attention. As she whipped her head to glare at him, she heard her name in Berta's high, warbling voice.

"Andrea, was there anything else you wanted to add?" Berta's look said she knew exactly what Andrea had been daydreaming about.

Now would be a good time to find a nice, deep hole to hide in for the next few months. Instead, she managed to shake her head. "Nothing now."

Berta simply nodded in a way that said she was holding her tongue, then the meeting concluded and everyone gathered their things to leave.

Andrea didn't move, even as Josh stood. He looked down at her. "You sure you're okay?"

"Yeah."

He settled back into his seat and angled to look at her, resting one arm on the back of their pew and one on the back of the pew in front of him, nearly enclosing her in a circle of lean muscle. "Thought you were hungry."

"I am." The group around them dispersed and chattered its way toward the door. "Just have a feeling I'll be interrogated if I get too close."

Question marks dotted Josh's face, then a knowing look slipped in and replaced whatever had him scowling in annoyance a few moments before. "Ah. You brought a boy to church. Inquiring minds want to know."

"Something like that. Past thirty and not married, you know. There's got to be something wrong with poor Andrea. Sorry, Josh. You're blood in the water and they're the circling sharks."

"It can't be that bad." Josh flashed a grin and leaned closer. As his lips nearly brushed her ear, sparks zipped across her jawline and into her lips. "The longer we sit in here and let them filter out that door, the more they're going to think something's up."

With effort, Andrea leaned away and met Josh's eyes. "And the more you whisper in my ear like that, the more they're going to talk."

The dark look shadowed his face again, then he seemed to remember where he was and shook his head. "You're right. Sorry." He stood and looked down at her. "I'd offer you my hand but then your friend at the back would think I was proposing marriage."

Andrea glanced over her shoulder to find Berta openly staring, not even pretending to hide her interest in the proceedings in the third pew.

Suddenly, Andrea didn't care anymore. Let people talk. Let them get the wrong idea. Or, the way Josh was sending signals this afternoon, maybe it was the right idea. It didn't matter. Like an irrational high schooler, more than anything in the world, she wanted her hand in his, by any means necessary. "Who cares?"

Josh stared down at her for a long time, then slowly held his hand out, palm up.

Andrea laced her fingers through his and let him pull her to her feet, then gripped tightly in case he had any ideas of letting go. So what if he was playacting? It felt so right. She'd deal with the jagged pieces of her broken heart later.

He shouldn't have done that. Now that Josh had Andrea's hand in his, he knew he'd taken a dive too far over the line to ever recover.

At the moment, he couldn't muster the will to care.

She laughed as soon as the church door closed behind them, but she didn't let go of his hand. "Thanks a lot. Now I'm going to be the center of attention at every meeting between now and the day Jesus steps foot back on this earth."

He squeezed her fingers and tried to ignore the way the slight breeze wisped the hair around her neck. "It's good for you. Builds character." Out of habit, he scanned the parking lot for anything out of place. It had become routine since they had started spending time together. He hadn't forgotten the trouble that stalked her; it never left his mind. Even though she was safe for the moment, he couldn't shake the feeling that if she got hurt on his watch, it would be his fault.

Nothing seemed out of place as they walked across the parking lot. A warm breeze blew through the pine trees and whispered that all was well. They'd found an oasis in the most clichéd place in the world: a churchyard.

Josh smiled at the sheer goofiness of the thought. It

was true. The woman messed with his head. "So. Lunch? I'm starving."

He expected her to hesitate. To pull her hand from his, retract her earlier invitation and claim she had paperwork to do. Instead, she flashed a smile that went all the way into her eyes. "Want to see if that Mexican restaurant over by the college is packed? We're way behind the rest of the church crowd now."

Josh glanced at his watch. "By the time we get over there, the church crowd will already be done eating."

Andrea started down the steps, tugging his hand. "Good. Let's go. I'll even let you drive."

She acted like this was a normal routine. His average Sunday included the occasional lunch out with his Sunday school class but, more often, it was bologna sandwiches and NASCAR races. This was infinitely better. He flashed a grin. "You seem less serious today."

"I can laugh or I can cry. And it's better to be smiling, because I never know when my picture's being taken." A frown pulled at her lips and she slipped her hand from his, stuffing it into the pocket of her capris. "They keep telling me to stop what I'm doing, to stop counseling soldiers. Why would they care? Although after Wade's relapse, maybe they're right."

Josh wished there was a way to kick himself. He should have known the question would lead her down a dark path. He shoved his hands into his own pockets and leaned against the door of his truck, watching a blue Mustang ease out of a space in the smaller parking lot on the other side of the church. "You need to stop considering yourself a failure. More than one therapist out there has had a patient relapse. I'm sure even psychiatrists on TV have that problem."

Andrea stopped tracing a crack in the pavement with

her toe. "Are you comparing me to a TV doctor?" The question dripped insult, but her eyes laughed.

"That's not a compliment?" He let himself sink into her gaze for a moment, but movement out of the corner of his eye jerked his attention from her.

The blue sports car in the far parking lot eased to a stop, and the passenger window slipped down.

Josh's eyes scanned the churchyard. No one had come out the door behind them. His flight response kicked in as he straightened. His practiced eyes took in the situation even as Andrea turned to see what had absorbed him.

"Josh? What's going—"

Without taking the time to think of what could happen if he were wrong, Josh hooked his arm around Andrea's waist and yanked her to the ground behind the truck as gunfire cracked an echo through the trees.

Andrea's forearm crashed into the back bumper of Josh's truck.

Another hard thump, and Josh roared like a wounded animal. Her head thudded into Josh's chest so hard that stars rushed through her vision. "Josh! What—" The words were cut off as he rolled over to cover her. Before any more thoughts could gel, she heard it. The silvery *thwack* of bullets tore the air and thudded into his truck.

She squeezed her eyes shut, memories of dusty buildings and sniper fire overtaking her, knocking her into a hazy place where she couldn't be sure what was real. *Dear God...get me out of this.* The squeal of rubber on pavement punctuated the air in a thin exclamation point, then there was nothing but silence.

The first sound she registered was her pulse pounding in her ears, then she heard Josh breathing hard against her back. Gravel dug into her cheek, and her arm throbbed where it had slammed into the truck. She tried to breathe, but her brain seemed unable to process oxygen and take inventory of her body at the same time. Other than her cheek and her arm, she felt no pain.

Air rushed into her lungs all at once as her body came back online, one function at a time. "Josh?"

His weight shifted from her back as he rolled away.

Andrea lifted her head as the shock wore off and her eyes focused. Josh lay on his back staring at the sky, eyes wide as he gripped his elbow and breathed as though he'd run full tilt up the side of Pine Mountain.

She pushed herself up, leaning over Josh, vaguely aware of familiar voices and approaching feet. Fear retreated as concern for him mounted. "Josh, look at me."

He stayed on his back, his face white beneath a red stain at his hairline. His breath shook as he exhaled. "You okay? Did they hit you?" The words washed over her with a warmth she couldn't interpret, not with her mind running from high to low speed like a poorly wound clock.

Josh lay still, his knuckles white as he gripped his arm. Her hand drifted toward his forehead, hovering halfway. She wasn't sure if she had the right to touch him or not. "You're bleeding."

Josh's eyes latched on to hers in a look that let her know her heart had definitely recovered from the fright. "Andrea—"

His words were swallowed by the remaining church members who surrounded them, pulling her to her feet, leading her away from him as sirens sounded in the distance. Where time had slowed moments before, it recovered and whipped by like those gunshots, leaving her with vague impressions of a blanket around her suddenly shaking shoulders, a fuzzy attempt to convince everyone she was fine and a once-over by a female paramedic who tried to talk her into a trip to the hospital.

On the church steps, Andrea brushed the medic off for the fourth time. “I’m fine. Really.” She flexed her arm and held it in the frustrated woman’s face. “It’s a bruise. I’m not injured. I’m not in shock.” She let her eyes drift over the paramedic’s shoulder to where Josh now sat, still on the ground behind his truck, surrounded by several EMTs who seemed to be in deep discussion with him. They blocked her full view, so she couldn’t see exactly what was happening.

The fear she swallowed had nothing to do with nearly being killed. “How is he?”

The paramedic looked over her shoulder as she wrapped the band around a blood pressure cuff before stowing it into her box. “I have no idea. I’ve been over here with you.”

Andrea bit her lower lip. “Sorry.”

“All I know is your hero didn’t take a bullet.” She turned back to Andrea, amusement and impatience tangling in the fine lines around her mouth. “From here, looks like something’s up with his elbow.”

“His elbow?” Andrea stood, her mouth slipping into a frown as the white emergency blanket slid from her shoulders. Surely not the elbow that had already ruined his life once before. “How bad?”

The woman shrugged. “Like I said, I’ve been busy with a patient refusing transport.”

“Thank you.” Andrea pulled the blanket the rest of the way from her shoulders and folded it over one arm, then held it out to the paramedic. “I mean that. Even if I am being difficult.”

The woman took the blanket, dropped it onto the bricks of the church steps and yanked at her graying brown ponytail. "Honey, you are nowhere near difficult." She jerked her head toward Josh. "It's fine if you go check on him. It's pretty clear to me where your heart is." She clicked the latches on her case and stood. "I'm fairly certain your arm isn't broken, but it's coming up a nasty bruise. If it gives you any kind of numbness or you think anything's wrong, you need to get it X-rayed." At Andrea's nod, she walked off toward the small cluster of emergency vehicles in the parking lot.

How did a stranger know where her heart was when Andrea didn't even know herself? Or at least she didn't want to admit it. The cold truth was, she'd been shot at where she should have been safe, where other people could have been hit, people she cared about. She'd be dead if it weren't for Josh. But the only thing she could think about, especially now that she knew all that he'd told her last night, was seeing for herself that he was really okay.

A vaguely familiar man wearing dark pants and a gray button-down shirt met her at the church steps. "Ms. Donovan? I'm Detective Martin."

"I'm sorry. I really can't think of anything other than what I've already told your people."

He waved her off and smiled, then gestured across the parking lot. "It's not me who has questions. The detective wants to talk to you when you're done."

Detective Simmons and two other policemen were speaking with Berta and the handful of other church members who had been in the building at the time of the shooting. Andrea had been told early on, after she questioned the paramedic, that no one else had been outside. The only casualty seemed to be Josh's pickup.

"Are you okay, ma'am?"

Andrea nodded, but her focus never left Josh. More

than she wanted to breathe, she needed to see that he was okay.

It seemed to take hours to cross the super-heated asphalt. By the time she made the trek, the paramedics had packed up their gear, and Josh was seated on the tailgate of the truck, his arm cradled in his lap, staring unseeing at the trees that ringed the property.

He didn't seem to notice Andrea until she stepped in front of him, then his eyes came into focus, even though no recognition lit his features. His lips pressed so tightly together the edges were white, and his forehead creased in pain.

Andrea patted the truck. "Mind if I sit? I think they're waiting to talk to us."

Josh nodded.

Andrea eased up onto the tailgate, trying to minimize the motion of the truck, but he flinched as she settled in. The expression twisted her heart. "You okay?"

He shrugged his good shoulder and continued to stare out at the woods. "They want me to go in and have my arm looked at."

"Are you?"

This time there was no acknowledgement at all. Josh hadn't been hit by any bullets that Andrea could tell, but something had certainly pierced his heart. She ached to climb over the wall that had been built in the past half hour, to get back to whatever was going on before another shadow could open fire.

Andrea sucked in a deep breath. *Open fire.* Someone had aimed a gun at her and pulled the trigger. This attack was more deliberate, more personal than any of the others. They knew where she went to church, knew when she'd be leaving...and they'd waited. The calculated, public nature of the violence said they wanted her, and they didn't care who else they took out in the process.

The quaking started in her chest and worked its way out until even her teeth knocked in staccato rhythm. She clamped her jaw tight and wrapped her arms around her stomach. This was nowhere near over. It had only just begun.

Josh wasn't looking at Andrea, but he sensed the instant the realization hit. When she'd walked over he knew that shock had kept her from understanding the situation, but when it struck, the truth came faster than any bullet. She was shaking so hard the tailgate of the truck rattled beneath him.

Sliding sideways, Josh bit back a groan as he lifted his good arm to wrap it around her shoulders, the motion pulling against the muscles in his back and reaching around to tear at his heart and remind him of his failures. He could not fail this time. Failure would mean losing Andrea, and that could not happen.

Josh froze into solid stone as Andrea shook against his chest. He couldn't love her, could not under any circumstances let himself feel this.

Even as he fought the shock, he knew. He knew why he'd never married anyone else, why he had left a string of three-date wonders behind him. Nobody was Andrea. And he'd loved her since the fall day she'd tripped past her brother's bedroom door and looked twice at him.

He pulled her close, determined to protect her against an unseen enemy, to get her life back onto level ground so he could confess and earn the right to tell her all of the things his heart had suddenly realized.

"This is never going to end, is it?" Her voice trembled.

"Yes, it will. I promise." If he had to die trying, he'd keep that promise.

"What did I do? Why me?"

A brusque new voice entered the conversation. "Well..."

Josh eased his head up to find Detective Simmons boring holes through Andrea with her gaze. Something about the set of her shoulders under a no-nonsense white button-down shirt said this was going to be an even tougher go-round than last time. He instinctively tightened his hold.

"That's what I want to find out, Ms. Donovan." The detective shifted her attention to Josh. "You're here again, I see."

Josh didn't respond. The question answered itself and was asked with such an air of annoyance he couldn't believe she'd bothered in the first place.

Shrugging one shoulder, Detective Simmons turned back to Andrea. "Any further contact with Wade Cameron?"

Josh's jaw tightened. Didn't this woman have any compassion? If Simmons weren't a cop, he'd step between her and Andrea and ask her to leave. If she weren't a cop and a woman, he'd step between her and Andrea and ask for a little heart-to-heart, in a man-to-man sort of way.

Andrea shook her head. "No."

"How about with the man who attacked you before?"

Eyes narrowing, Josh jerked his head up. "You mean the man you told us was in custody yesterday when you assured us Andrea was safe? Check your cameras at the jail. She hasn't had any contact."

Something like approval flickered across the detective's face, but it was gone before he could fully identify it. "Looks like this is bigger than we thought." She clicked her pen a few times, waiting so that the slight breeze through the pines punctuated her pause. "You're keeping something from me, Ms. Donovan. If we're going to catch the people behind this, you'll have to tell us everything you know. Now, have you seen Wade Cameron again?"

The hesitation in Andrea flowed through to Josh. There was an instant when her breath actually stopped, and it stretched out so long he thought he'd have to shake her. He knew what she was thinking, knew she wondered if what they'd found constituted contact.

Finally, she drew in a breath. "No."

"But we found something." His admission came so quickly it surprised him.

Andrea's shoulders stiffened beneath his arm, and he wondered if it was shock or betrayal.

It took all of three seconds for Detective Simmons to register the words and turn to him. "What's that?"

When Josh slipped his arm from Andrea's shoulder to pull his phone from his hip pocket, she slid away. Betrayal. They'd agreed not to share the information until they knew what it was, and he'd unilaterally decided to break that agreement. Livid wouldn't come close to describing his reaction if she'd done this to him. Resigned to the fate he'd created, Josh clicked through the texts on his phone with his left hand, then held it out to the detective.

She hesitated. "You're not usually left-handed, are you, First Sergeant?"

He shook his head.

"You were hurt today?"

Andrea breathed in sharply. Had she not noticed before?

"Old injury. From college." They could leave it at that. He flicked a gaze to Andrea, who regarded him with hooded eyes. She'd retreated to a place he couldn't reach and seemed to be warring with herself about whether she wanted to stay there or not.

It was probably better if she stayed there. He'd only let her down again if she placed any more trust in him.

Simmons took the phone and drew him back into the present. "Care to explain?"

Josh laid out everything that had happened last night while the detective noted it and called over a uniformed officer to coordinate with post and retrieve the only real evidence they had.

As the detective talked with the other officers, Josh completely checked out of the conversation, the personal implications of this latest attack setting in. He still reeled not only from the pain in his arm but from the knowledge he loved Andrea, that last night's kiss hadn't been a fluke.

And look what that kiss had done, his mind chided him. It had lulled him into complacency, made him forget everything he'd ever learned about combat. When things looked the quietest, that's when a soldier had to be on the highest alert. He'd dismissed the photo from the previous night as unimportant, a tactical error that had nearly killed them both. His emotions had taken over, and because he'd failed to be vigilant, he'd failed her.

He couldn't let that happen again. Still, as horrible a job as he was doing at shielding her from danger, he knew there was no one else who could step in and do it. It was all on him. And the only way to protect her was to back away emotionally and do his job.

Even if it broke his heart.

The conversation between Josh and Detective Simmons buzzed in Andrea's ears like aggravated hornets, and it made about as much sense. The sounds wouldn't form into coherent sentences.

Josh. Injured. Protecting her. She'd known he was hurt, but the extent hadn't really sunk in until the detective asked him about it. Now the possibilities swirled like a hurricane.

He'd made that dive to protect her. If any of those bullets had veered a few inches, Josh would have been the one they hit.

Lost in what-ifs, Andrea pressed her fingers to her mouth and battled the most abject terror she'd felt yet. Nausea rode shuddering waves through her stomach, burned her throat and tightened her lungs. She couldn't put him in that kind of position again.

"I want protection." She blurted the request before she could change her mind.

Josh's head came up like she'd landed an uppercut to his jaw. "What?"

Detective Simmons stopped in midsentence and turned to Andrea. She regarded her for a long time before dipping her head in a nod. "That's the smartest thing I've heard you say yet, Ms. Donovan, and I wish I could offer you that, but..." She drew a breath that spoke of regret. "We don't have those kinds of resources. There might be other options we can look into, though."

Josh didn't seem to hear the detective's words. He stared at Andrea until she met his gaze. When she did, it was like someone pulled the curtains shut in a brightly lit house. Where the man she thought she'd known once sat, a stranger stepped in and regarded her with an expression devoid of emotion.

It was better that way. The less he felt for her, the easier this would be. He'd be safer without her near. And while she might not be able to save herself, she could at least get Josh out of the line of fire.

ELEVEN

Two o'clock in the morning. The numbers on the microwave shone brighter than usual in the darkness of his kitchen. How many times would Josh see that number creep around on the dial before this was all over? He chased two ibuprofen with milk and leaned against the counter, cradling his arm against his stomach. Still, the pain in his arm couldn't compare with the one in his heart. That pain shot fire along every nerve ending.

The few times he'd managed to catch sleep tonight, he'd sat straight up gasping out of nightmares painted with burning vehicles and futile efforts at salvation.

In the fiery visions, unlike reality, Andrea was trapped in the flames while he fought helplessly and failed.

The real Andrea, the one who lived and breathed and tapped on the locked door of his heart, knew he was a failure. She'd reared back and slapped him full force this afternoon by asking for protection. She knew he couldn't do it, didn't trust him to keep her away from harm.

Josh winced against the dual pain. Smart girl.

He hadn't done her any favors by violating their agreement to remain silent about what they knew, either. In hindsight, not taking the panel to the police in the first place was one of their bigger mistakes, but he couldn't bear to think they'd turn accusing eyes on her again.

He'd messed up. There hadn't been a moment since he'd laid eyes on her that he'd done things right. Josh ran his left hand over two days' worth of stubble, and groaned. If he was so bad for her, why did he want to pick up the phone and hear her voice?

Because he was long gone over her. Seventeen years long gone. His inattention on the baseball field because of her presence had gotten him into trouble more than once. Time hadn't diminished her ability to distract him from what was important.

Tight, aggravated muscles pulled all the way into his neck as Josh stretched his arm. He had thanked God more than once over the course of this long night that he hadn't broken it again. That kind of re-injury probably would have ended his future in the army the same way the first go-round had tanked his baseball career and shattered his childhood dreams.

Crazy thing was, as much as the sport had been the air he breathed all the way up into college, once he joined the army he'd never missed it. Pickup games were enough to satisfy the itch to get a glove on every once in a while, even if he couldn't throw the way he used to. That was the kind of healing only God could do.

When Brendan died, he realized alcohol wouldn't kill the pain and turned back to Christ, had let Him come in and heal him. Forgiveness had been easy to find. Release had not. While the pain had eased, the knowledge that he'd let two people die never left. He could never let his guard down or the same thing might happen again.

And there had always been a cavern in his soul, something that gnawed like hunger, even when he tried to fill it. God had poured so much into him, it seemed there shouldn't be room left for anything else.

Light from the refrigerator cast a surreal glow over the kitchen as he poured another glass of milk. He shut the door, then drained the glass and clinked it into the sink. For a while, he'd thought the hole in his life—the one he'd tried to fill with work and every army course possible—had to do with losing baseball. Tonight, there was no denying it. Now that Andrea had dug into his heart and taken up residence there, he knew that void had more to do with having somebody to come home to, somebody besides his mother to send him care packages overseas, somebody to miss him and to give him a reason to come back.

There was a reason he'd become a confirmed bachelor. He couldn't bear the burden of someone else's welfare. What if he failed again, this time with someone he loved?

He clicked his tongue and ran it along the back of his teeth. *Face it, Walker.* He was past gone, already in love with Andrea. Always had been.

Resigning himself to wakefulness, he padded across the room in bare feet and raised the blinds to stare at the driveway. A rental car sat there, taunting him. The cops had hauled his truck away to dig the bullets out of it. They could keep it, for all he cared. Even repaired, it would only be one more reminder of how the woman he loved had almost died under his care.

He lowered his head against the glass, barely cooled from the heat of the day. The fact that he was a fraud when it came to protecting the people around him had never weighed heavier. He'd failed so many people so many times.

Who?

The question wasn't audible, but it was so close that he jerked his head up to make sure he was still alone.

Who exactly have you failed?

Brendan, for telling him they could talk "later." Lauren. If he'd had a better grip on the wheel, had checked his tire pressure, had worn his seat belt and not been thrown from the car…

Then he'd be dead, too. Unable to help her then. Unable to help Andrea today. Andrea, who he'd also failed…

How?

Josh braced both hands against the window frame and gripped the wood until his knuckles ached and his elbow protested. How had he failed her?

He hadn't. He squeezed his eyes tight as the revelation crashed against layers of habitual self-recrimination. The images of his charred SUV faded away, overwritten by a new film. The attack at the counseling center. The perceived threat at his unit. The gunshots at the church. He swallowed hard. Each time, Andrea had needed him… and he'd come through. Had not failed.

How long had he been worshipping the idol of himself, focusing solely on his own strength? What was it his preacher had quoted from Psalms? *Through You we push back our enemies; through Your name we trample our foes.* Not by his power. God's. Not his weakness but God's strength.

It wasn't his might that did anything, and if he kept holding on, God would never be able to take care of anything. He had to let go. Had to give up control. Had to take a risk.

And he knew without a doubt where his first step would take him.

Twenty-four hours ago, holding the bottom of a metal locker in her hands, Andrea had felt like she and Josh could do anything. Now, huddled in the corner of her couch in the dark, she wondered if she'd ever see him again.

While she'd been answering even more of the detective's questions at the church, Josh had slipped from sight. When the flatbed showed up to haul his truck away, he was nowhere to be found. Whatever had died in his eyes this afternoon had been because of her. She'd kept him from further danger, but something told her he'd read the act as rejection. If she explained her actions, he'd be right back here, doing his level best to stand in front of any fist or bullet that had her name on it.

This admission cut worse than the night Brendan figured out her crush and told her she'd never have a chance with a guy like Josh. The same night he told her Josh was taking Amy Phipps to the senior prom.

To this day, Andrea couldn't stand Amy Phipps. The girl had never said two words to her, but Andrea still couldn't get over believing they were mortal enemies. Despite the ache in her gut, she grinned at the immaturity. Someday maybe she'd grow up. Most of the time, she rather doubted it.

The light in the room shifted and grew darker. Without even looking at the clock, Andrea knew it wouldn't be long until the sun cracked the horizon. She'd seen enough predawns to know the old adage was true. It really was darkest right before dawn. If that were the case, maybe light would come back into her life soon. It sure couldn't get much blacker than this.

For the fifteenth time since she woke up a little after two, she pulled out her cell phone and toyed with the idea of dialing Josh's number. Not at this time of day. Maybe tomorrow. Maybe never. It was doubtful he ever wanted to hear from her again, anyway. The conspicuous absence of his vehicle from the parking lot below testified to that.

Instead, she clicked to her photos and enlarged the one she'd kept of the wall locker. The detective had erased the pictures on Josh's phone but hadn't realized Andrea possessed a copy. She felt a little guilty about having evidence she shouldn't, but the actual locker floor had been turned over to the police, so there couldn't be any real harm in looking at a photo.

Guilt pushed Andrea to set the phone aside. She kneaded the bridge of her nose with her thumb and index finger. Since when did she become an armchair detective who believed she knew more than the police? It would be better if they handled the sleuthing while she focused on keeping herself alive one more day.

Something slipped against her apartment door. A slight rustle, then silence.

Andrea sat straighter and dropped her feet lightly to the floor. Someone was out there. Gripping her phone, she eased across the carpet to the door, careful to avoid the creaky spot on the small hardwood entry, and cautiously leaned forward to peer through the peephole, hoping it was true that no one could see in from the other side.

A soft knock nearly threw her backward, a light shriek ripping from her throat as her phone clattered across the floor and came to a swift halt under a table against the edge of the beige carpet.

"Andrea." Her name passed through the door.

On hands and knees she scrambled for the phone, until the voice came again.

"It's me."

Her muscles froze as her fingertips grasped the phone, and she dropped back, staring at the steel door. Her pulse raced twice as fast as it had when she thought a random intruder lurked outside.

"Josh?" His name squeaked out, and she cleared her

throat. Her voice needed to be strong, authoritative, to make him leave before he could get hurt again. "What are you doing here?"

"I needed to see you."

That did it. Emotion overtook reason and she rose to her feet, flicked the deadbolt and opened the locked door she'd hidden behind since he kissed her.

Josh stood in the dim light of the passageway, seeming hesitant to cross the threshold.

The sight of him in navy basketball shorts and a gray T-shirt with the old infantry "Follow Me" logo on it made her grip the doorknob harder. He looked like the young Josh, the one that never left her memory. How did he do that? Make the space between her old crush and her new feelings fold over themselves in emotional origami?

"Did something happen?" There had to be a reason he'd shown up here unannounced, in such a rush he hadn't even combed his hair. It rumpled across his head like he'd run his hand back through it more than once on the way to her apartment.

"I needed to see you," he repeated. The uncertainty rolled off him like steam on asphalt after a summer storm.

The heat that still lingered in the outside stairwell drifted into the apartment around him in a way that left her unsure if it came from the outside world or from whatever crackled between them.

She took a step back to give him room to pass. "Because I'm in more danger than we thought?"

Her question seemed to release the brakes that held him in place. Stepping through the door he met her toe-to-toe, looking down at her, his nose scant inches from hers. "Because of you."

How was she supposed to respond to that?

It didn't matter if she had a response or not. Josh

slipped his left hand behind her neck and pulled her close, his mouth hovering near hers as though he waited for permission.

In response, she closed the gap, wrapping her arms around his neck and meeting him halfway in a moment that drove Saturday's kiss from her mind. This was not a throwback to a high school dream. This was an entirely new thing, a fresh realization that the man in front of her was everything but a memory.

It was simultaneously seconds and years when they pulled apart, Josh resting his forehead against hers.

Andrea drew a shallow breath. "Do you regret doing that?"

"Do you?"

She shook her head slightly, and he slipped his hand down her arm to squeeze her fingers before he pulled away. "Then we need to talk." The low rumble of authority in his voice sent warm shivers across her stomach. She was not standing in front of a man who was about to renege on his actions again.

"I'm sorry I barged in on you like that." Josh wandered to the window and peeked out, keeping his back to her.

"I'm not." A nervous laugh escaped her. "I just…" She fluttered her hands when he turned back to look at her. "What brought that on?"

Josh threw his head back and exhaled loudly, exposing his Adam's apple.

Don't go there. Andrea forced herself into sanity before she planted a kiss where there was no permission to go. She had a feeling they were treading rocky ground in more ways than one, that this moment might be more dangerous than any they'd faced in the past few days.

When he lowered his eyes to hers, she saw a new resolve shining at her. "You said I was hiding something."

The weight of unspoken truth sank Andrea to the edge of the couch. This was it, the thing that stood between them. Instinctively, she knew it would either draw them together or rip them apart. She pulled a throw pillow against her stomach and gripped it like a shield.

"My accident? It was the same night Brendan died."

Her brows furrowed. Why would he hide that?

"But it's not the whole reason I wasn't at the funeral." With a long breath, he came back and dropped to the ottoman in front of her, his knees hovering close to hers without touching. "Brendan showed up at my door that night, wanting to hang out, and I told him it would have to be later because I had a date."

It took a second for the words to weave into a coherent pattern. Brendan went to Josh. Josh turned him away. If Josh had set aside his plans…

"I know," he said. "Believe me, I know. If I'd stood up Lauren for him, they'd both still be alive."

Andrea's hands went to her lips as she slid back and broke contact. "You turned him away when he was in trouble?"

"No." Josh pulled her hands from her face, wrapping her icy fingers in his warmth. She didn't want him to touch her, but she was powerless to pull free. "He wasn't in trouble. He was discharged from the army, thinking about coming to school, wanted to see if I thought he had a prayer of playing ball if he came in as an older freshman."

"He was talking about the future?"

"He was. And when I told him there was a girl—" Josh swallowed hard "—he said he'd heard there was a party happening across campus and he'd see me there later." He slipped closer, his voice low and urgent. "I think the overdose was an accident. It had to be. Nobody who talks like he did ends his life just a few hours later."

Answers. How long had he held the answers her family wanted so desperately? "Were you ever going to tell us? All this time we wondered, and you kept it from us." She jerked her hands away, but his grip tightened.

"Up until tonight, I was convinced I'd killed them both. That it was my fault. Until I saw you again, it never crossed my mind that you didn't know he didn't intend to die. Until tonight, it was all about me. I admit that. I couldn't see outside of myself to realize other people were hurting. My head knew it, but my heart didn't."

Training kicked in, masking her emotions. "Survivor guilt." Just like her own guilt. In spite of everything, in spite of the hatred and anger she wanted to feel, Josh's former words rose up. "You didn't fail him. Or Lauren. You had no way of knowing what would happen to either of them."

"I know that now."

"And you didn't fail me, either."

His fingers squeezed tighter. "I don't—"

The chime of an incoming text message stopped him.

Josh pulled his phone from his pocket, regret seeping into his expression. Surprise overtook his other emotions and he rose, breaking the connection between them. "It's Cameron."

Andrea's heart fluttered between disappointment and shock. "Why is he texting you?"

"All of my soldiers have my number." He scrolled the message. "He wants to see you."

"Then why not call me?"

"Does he have your personal number?"

Good point. "When?"

Josh took a step back and flashed the screen at her. "As soon as possible. At the counseling center. You should call Detective Simmons."

"And scare Wade off?" The kid was so skittish he'd run if he caught sight of anything out of place, and then they'd be right back where they'd started. "Josh, if we've got a prayer of stopping this, we've got to keep him in one place long enough to tell me the truth about what's going on. I'm meeting him. Now. And I'm not taking the police."

"You're not going alone. I'll drive. That kid might be scrawny, but he's strong, and if he doesn't show up alone or this is some sort of trick..." He headed for the door with long strides. His hand was on the doorknob before he turned to face her. "I'm not losing you now."

TWELVE

Of all the dumb chances he'd ever taken, this may well rank up there with the absolute dumbest. And it wasn't his life he was messing with.

It was Andrea's.

For the twenty-seventh time since they'd left her apartment, Josh checked the rearview mirror to see if anyone had followed them. He felt only slightly safer driving an anonymous rental car than he did driving his pickup, but there was no telling what their faceless enemy knew or where they lurked. His left hand gripped the wheel, his right elbow resting on the console, pain pulsing with each heartbeat.

Beside him, Andrea puffed out a deep breath and leaned her head against the seat back. In spite of everything, she wasn't scanning the road around them, wasn't looking for danger. She'd climbed in the car without question, laid her life in his hands and assumed he was man enough to handle the situation.

In the wake of what he'd confessed just moments before, her level of undeserved trust gripped Josh's heart. His grasp on the steering wheel tightened. "I'm sorry."

There was a slight rustle as she shifted in her seat. "For what?"

"Everything."

Oncoming headlights played on her face for what seemed like forever while she thought. "My brother battled things in his head that I'll never understand, things he was powerless to control by himself. Even if you'd broken your promise to Lauren and been there with him that night, you probably wouldn't have been able to stop him. He tried to fix what was broken by himself. He made his own choices." She cleared her throat. "Maybe I'm starting to see that for the first time."

"A tough lesson coming out of the chaos you're in."

"Maybe." She planted her feet in the floorboard and pushed back into the seat. "I should be the one apologizing. You probably thought I was pushing you away when I was trying to protect you yesterday."

"What?" Where was this little bit of information earlier? Her revelation would have caused him to run right off the road if he hadn't been holding the wheel so tightly. "Trying to protect me? From what?"

"From them. You nearly got killed because of me. I couldn't live with myself if something happened to you."

Oh, how he wanted to pursue that. If things were different, he'd pull over right now and they'd hash out every emotion building in this relationship.

But now wasn't the time. Rather than follow this line of conversation down its inevitable road, Josh ignored the pain in his elbow and reached over to brush the hair from her face, tucking it behind her ear. "How much sleep did you get before I showed up?"

She stiffened, then received his gesture as an acceptance of her apology and allowed him to change the subject. "Counting the thirty seconds I just catnapped?" A smile flickered on her face in the pink light of predawn. "About thirty seconds. You?"

"You beat me by a whopping twelve seconds." Josh relaxed into the seat. Only a handful of headlights shone in the rearview mirror along 185 on this early morning. None seemed suspicious. "Any oh-dark-thirty theories on what Cameron's little wall locker code might mean?"

Andrea didn't answer. Her breathing had fallen into the even, shallow rise and fall of sleep.

Josh smiled and let her doze. Soon enough he'd have to wake her up and face whatever it was that Cameron had for them. They'd need to be on top of their game.

Not for the first time, he rethought the decision to go meet him without notifying the police. Uniforms could have stayed far enough back not to arouse Cameron's flight response, and it would have made Josh feel a whole lot better to know someone besides him had Andrea's back. Someone with guns.

His phone rested in the cup holder between the seats. He really should call Detective Simmons. The woman was probably sound asleep, but chances were she'd had more rest than the occupants of this car combined and could have a team in place in the next ten minutes, before he and Andrea even hit the Victory Drive exit.

"Don't even think about it," Andrea muttered.

A quick glance showed her eyes still closed.

"You already handed over our one link to whoever's doing this to us." She sat up in the seat and stretched her arms over her head, words drowning in a yawn. "If he takes off scared again, chances are he's not coming back, and then we've got nothing." She dropped her hand to the side of the seat and it rested there, taunting him, daring him to reach over and pick it up.

Fourteen years in the military and he couldn't keep himself more vigilant than this? It was foolish to approach her when she was still in danger, to let his emotions take control the way they had tonight. He should go back through basic training and learn a little more discipline. Then her words filtered into his consciousness. "Our link to whoever is doing this to *us?*" She thought of them as a team.

"He's your soldier. And it seems like that last shot wasn't aimed solely at me." She drew her eyebrows tight. "No pun intended."

Andrea was more nervous than it seemed if she was walking the fine line between humor and sarcasm again. Forget every alarm screaming in his head. He eased his hand over and wrapped his fingers around hers. "It's going to be okay." He hoped his words sounded more convincing to her than they did to him.

"If I didn't believe that, I'd walk up the middle of Veterans Parkway at high noon and let them wipe me out. It would be a whole lot better than looking over my shoulder for the rest of my life."

Josh squeezed her hand one more time and let go, even though he wanted to hold on like a lifeline. "Let's hope it doesn't come to that. There's too much left for us to talk about yet."

Silence settled in again as they passed the airport, runway lights glistening like Christmas in July. "Josh?"

He studied the lines on the road before he answered. The tone of her voice set his guard high. "Yeah?"

"Why did you pick tonight to tell me?"

The soft question coupled with several days' worth of no sleep loosened the gag on his typically guarded emotions. "I've carried that with me for years, and it stood between us. I had to know if it would make you walk, had to get it out of the way. I don't want to lose you. Not now." He fell silent, the only sound the hum of the wheels on the road. "And here I've dragged you out without any backup. You keep me from thinking straight."

Andrea remained quiet, and Josh wondered what was going through her head. Finally, she said, "You're trying to make atonement. That's why you're here."

"If you'd have said that yesterday, I'd have agreed. I fully believed it was my fault Lauren and Brendan died and now God wanted me to make it right." Josh squeezed the steering wheel, choking the voice of the old lie that threatened to creep up once again. "Now I'm here because I want to be. We've come too far for me to walk out on you now."

Another car appeared behind them, and Josh slipped back into the moment at hand, whipping off at Victory Drive without using the blinker. The other car slipped past on the way to post. "Far as I can tell, nobody's following us."

"That's good. But what's waiting for us when we get there?"

She fidgeted with the door locks, then opened and closed the glove box, all nervous energy. "I never dreamed I'd see a day when I was afraid to go to my own office." She sat back in her seat, fingering the hem of her pale gray workout shirt.

Without taking his eyes off the road, Josh reached over and took her hand again, determined not to let go. "It's going to be okay."

As soon as he touched her, she stilled. "I'm choosing to believe you."

The next couple of minutes passed in silence. Josh fought hard to keep his foot even on the gas pedal. He wanted to slow down and take in every bit of the surroundings, but creeping along the nearly deserted road would make them stand out like a rookie in Fenway Park on opening day.

Beside him, Andrea leaned forward, gripping his hand tightly as the parking lot came into view. “Empty.” She sat back as they slowed. “He’s not here.”

Josh slowed the car early and pulled into the gas station next door, parking near the road. He let go of her hand to switch off the engine and fought the intense urge to pick it up again.

“What are we doing?” She sat back and clasped her hands between her knees.

“If we pull up over there, any interested party who drives by is going to know exactly who we are. We sit here, maybe it won’t be so noticeable.” He tapped the screen of his phone. “I still think we should call—”

“I want this over with, and if it means I have to do something reckless, well then, call me reckless.” She turned to stare at the gas pumps, treating Josh to a view of the back of her head. “Besides, I’ve got you on my side.”

Her words struck Josh somewhere between his rib cage and his heart, like a line drive he once took to the chest. It had knocked the wind out of him and laid him flat on his back, filling his vision with blue sky and black spots until he could get a good breath again. He swallowed the old habit of telling her again how wrong she was to trust him. Closing the space between them, he ran his fingers through the back of her hair, separating the waves and wrapping one ringlet around his index finger. It was softer than he’d expected. “I’m not going anywhere until this is over or God says my part in it’s done.” He surprised himself by believing the words.

Andrea turned, trapping his fingers in the curls at the base of her neck. When her eyes met his, every ounce of exhaustion faded into the background, every bit of caution faded. His fingers tightened reflexively as if they were afraid she'd pull back and force him to let go.

"Josh, I… You're…" The whispered words sparked electricity into the air.

Josh didn't really hear what she said, he was so caught up in the way her lips moved. The upholstery of the seats rustled beneath them as he awkwardly pulled her closer with his left arm and leaned to meet her halfway.

She didn't resist. But just as he could feel her breath against his lips, she tensed and scrambled backward, tearing his hand from her hair and fumbling for the door.

Had she lost her mind? "Don't go charging—" The door slammed behind her, and she took off at a run. At first, he thought the mad dash was to get away from him, but then he saw the man skulking toward her building.

Pressed backward into his seat by the danger and helpless to do anything from where he sat, Josh reached for the door handle and hit the ground running.

"Dutch!" Andrea shouted across the space between them, realizing too late she'd just exposed herself to anyone who might be watching.

The older man stopped in the middle of the parking lot, twisting like he was going to bolt across Victory Drive and into the tree line on the other side of the road.

Andrea jogged toward him, gulping deep breaths and fighting to regain her footing.

Even though she was completely out in the open right now, her priority was getting Dutch out of harm's way. If something happened to anyone else because of her, she'd give up without a fight.

When she reached Dutch, he tucked his fist into his oversize coat pocket like a kid caught with his hand in the cookie jar.

Alarm bells shot off in Andrea's ears and all thoughts of angry assailants fled. She propped her hands on her knees and tried to catch her breath. "Tell me—" she gulped in a breath "—tell me I didn't just catch you drinking."

Confusion scattered across his face before his usual open expression set in. "I'm a better man than that, Miss Andrea." Lines tightened his face, and he shoved his hands into his coat pockets as footsteps pounded the pavement behind her.

Josh drew up beside her and asked Dutch, "What are you doing here?"

Dutch took a step back and eyed the younger man warily. "You're still here?"

Josh flicked a look at Andrea and directed the question to her. "Tell me again why you trust him?"

Andrea finally caught her breath and straightened, thinking irrationally that she sure wasn't in the shape she used to be in if she couldn't sprint two hundred yards without her lungs burning. "He's safe." She shoved her hair behind her ears and looked toward Josh, although she couldn't quite meet his eyes, too afraid of what she'd see there.

Josh nodded at Dutch before he spoke to Andrea. "Don't you think it's a little less than smart to be standing here in the middle of the great wide open?"

"Why would it be dangerous to stand in her own parking lot?" Dutch's ears practically perked up. "I knew it. I knew something was going on." He gripped Andrea's arm, and Josh stiffened beside her. "They came back after you, didn't they? Those guys who were here the other night. They're why I've been hanging around more this weekend, checking the place out to make sure it's safe."

Andrea laid a hand on his and gently loosened his fingers from her wrist. "You can see for yourself I'm fine but Dutch, I need you to get somewhere else right now. The last place you want to be is anywhere near me. Especially out in the open like this." She dropped her hand and turned at a sharp angle, making for the relative safety of her office, praying no one was pulling surveillance on her building.

"Miss Andrea!" A new voice bounced off the brick building.

Her fists balled against the cotton of her yoga pants. *No. No. No. Not one more person to be hurt. Please.* She turned. "Mr. Miller, you have to go back to the store. Now." At best, Wade was going to run for the hills when he saw the parade trailing her. At worst, someone would die in the next two minutes.

The cup of coffee in Mr. Miller's hand dipped with the corners of his mouth as he huffed to a stop. "I'm sorry. Did I do something wrong?"

"You didn't do anything. But please. Go back into your store where it's safe." Andrea turned to Josh as the stronger of the two of them, begging him silently to intervene.

"Sir, it's best if you go. Now."

A scowl whispered across Mr. Miller's face before he sighed. "Is this about what happened the other day?"

Andrea hesitated before she nodded.

"Then I'm calling the police." Before Andrea could stop him, he turned and pulled his cell phone from his pocket, lumbering away faster than Andrea thought the little round man possibly could.

She moved to go after him, but Josh grabbed her wrist. "It's too late, anyway. If Cameron saw any of this, he's already long gone."

This was it. The stress of carrying everyone else's lives on her shoulders was three seconds from splitting her in two. A dull pain gouged at her temple, threatening to force tears. If some shadowy person wanted her to stop doing what she loved, fine. But she couldn't hold up any longer, couldn't watch any more people place themselves in the crosshairs. "I quit. I'll give them what they want. They want the file? They want me to stop counseling? I'll shut down. They win."

"You quit what?" Josh grasped her shoulders. "Stop it. You can't let them do this to you."

Dutch stepped up, reminding her he hadn't left yet. "I'm not sure what all is happening here or who *they* is, but I've got your back. And I think this boy here does, too. Don't let a few bad apples steal what you're doin' here, Doc."

Her head ached with the tension of decision. "Just leave me alone." Turning on her heel, she practically marched toward the front door. There was no reason to look back to know that both men followed her. Josh's purposeful, precise step and Dutch's slight shuffle kept time with her.

Her hand was in her pocket for the keys when Josh gripped her upper arm and dragged her backward to a stop. Her back collided with the solid wall of his chest and, despite the situation swirling around them, she definitely noticed.

For a few breaths, he held her tight against him, then leaned down to whisper against her ear. "Your friend is carrying a weapon."

Andrea's heart did its best to squeeze between her ribs. It was a fight for her next inhaled breath. Josh had to be wrong. Why would a guy like Dutch need to carry? Where would he even get a gun? Once again, the world tilted, and everything she knew to be true was distorted as though reflected in a fun-house mirror.

Dutch stood too close for Andrea to ask questions.

From this angle, she couldn't read either man's face but knowing Josh, a plan already whirled in his head.

Before she could react, Josh released her and spun on Dutch, backing the older man against the large window at the front of the counseling center, his left forearm to Dutch's neck, right arm tucked protectively close to his side.

Dutch's eyes hardened in that initial instant as Andrea gasped and stepped back, torn between shielding herself and defending her friend. As she watched, the mask slipped into place, and shock tinged Dutch's expression.

Josh pressed farther, forcing Dutch's chin up. "Who are you, really?"

"I'm…I'm me. I'm Dutch. Just a homeless guy." His gaze shifted frantically to Andrea. "Tell him who I am, Doc."

Andrea couldn't even move. The whole scene was so incongruous to everything she thought of as reality.

"Don't talk to her." Josh leaned in closer. "Talk to me. Your average homeless guy doesn't carry a gun. It wouldn't be allowed in any shelter I know of."

"I'm not—"

"You are. I saw it ten seconds ago when you reached up to shift your ball cap."

A car engine hummed closer across the parking lot. Andrea swallowed hard against a rising tide of new panic. "Josh. It's Detective Simmons and another police car."

Josh didn't even look her way. "Good. She can deal with your friend."

Detective Simmons stepped out of her car and stood behind the door, surveying the scene. "What's going on here?"

"He's got a weapon."

"I don't have no weapon. And he assaulted me." Dutch

was suddenly all motion, fighting Josh. "I didn't do nothing. Arrest him."

The detective stepped closer. Her eyes narrowed, and she reached toward Dutch with the swiftness of a striking snake. When her hand reappeared, a gun came with it.

Andrea gasped and stepped back as Josh tightened his grip against the older man, eliciting a grunt.

"So this isn't yours? You tripped and it fell into your waistband?"

Lines appeared around Dutch's eyes and mouth, but he said nothing.

"Okay, fine." Simmons handed the gun off to a nearby officer and pulled out a pair of handcuffs. "Unless you can produce a concealed-carry permit, you're under arrest."

Andrea's fingers chilled as Josh stepped back and an officer hauled Dutch past her. He never even looked in her direction.

"Now..." The detective turned her attention back to Andrea. "Mind telling me why the two of you are here? Seems like an odd place for breakfast."

Andrea straightened her shoulders. "Do you want to accuse me of something else?"

A summons from the officer who had custody of Dutch stopped whatever Simmons was going to say next. She turned and followed them, speaking over her shoulder as she stepped from the sidewalk to the pavement. "We'll find out if he's one of the men trying to harm you. Until then, go home. We'll talk about what you were doing here later."

"She's right." Josh gripped Andrea's elbow. "All of this activity likely scared Wade away, anyway."

Pressing a finger to her lips, Andrea nodded and watched the police car pull out of the parking lot. She felt trapped in a whirlwind of events blowing by in mere seconds. Had the man she'd trusted so completely been about to kill her?

THIRTEEN

The car ride back to her apartment bogged down in a silence so heavy it blocked every effort to dispel it. If she listened hard enough, the car's engine probably revved higher under the added weight of her spirit.

Dutch. Armed and present when he'd never been to her office on a Monday before. If he was truly guilty, then no one in her life was above suspicion. As far as Andrea was concerned, Dutch's arrest was one more betrayal in a growing mountain of lies. Had he been snooping in her office, going through her stuff under the guise of helping? Her entire life felt like an illusion.

Maybe she was dreaming. Hopefully she'd wake up soon and find out all of this was the result of bad Chinese food before bed.

Except Josh. If only she could banish the rest of her life as a nightmare and keep him. It had been so long since anyone had gotten close, and he'd managed to kick down the barriers she'd built like they were made of a child's wooden blocks. Her entire life since her brother's death had been dedicated to helping soldiers like him, the wounded who came back with scars no one could see, who self-medicated until they could care less whether or not they ever felt again. For the first time, Andrea was tired of doing it alone.

"There something on my cheek?" Josh's words cut the threads of her twisted musings.

It took a second for her to remember where she was. "What?"

"You were staring at me." Though he didn't turn to her, his expression held a slight amusement, like he'd been able to read her mind.

"Actually, I wasn't even seeing you." Not really. "My mind was somewhere else." Great. Now he'd want to know where it was. She turned her attention back out the window and shrugged, hoping he'd buy her nonchalance. "I think I'll see about getting a window in my office." She turned her gaze out the side window.

Josh clicked the blinker to get off the highway at her exit. "So you're not giving up the center after all?"

"No. I'm not. Whatever is going on, I won't fail my brother or anybody else who's dealing with that pain. I can't." Seeing Dutch hauled away hadn't dimmed that passion. It had only stoked a new blaze of determination. "No matter what any two-bit criminals try to throw at me, keeping that place open is what I'm supposed to do."

"And the window?"

"When I leased the building, I thought not having one added privacy. Lately, with all that's happened, it just feels like the walls are closing in."

"That sounds like it's got more to do with your life than your office."

"True." Andrea sniffed and dragged her index finger along the edge of the window, fine dust smudging her fingertip. "So Dutch has been up to something this whole time."

"Nobody said that." Josh's voice fell flat. "He could be

carrying that pistol for protection. It's likely it had nothing to do with you. He probably sleeps under a bridge at night. Without it, he could be dead."

"You sure didn't seem to trust him earlier."

"I don't trust anybody who's armed around you right now. But I'm saying you can't jump to conclusions. He could just as easily be innocent of any of this."

"He could be." She was powerless to stop the sarcasm from tingeing her words. "But it doesn't do a thing to keep me from wondering who else is lying to me. Or about me." She tossed a hand in his direction.

"I haven't lied to you."

Her reply congealed and stuck in her throat. The comment was too intimate for the moment, loaded with subtext and emotion. It took a second for her muscles to loosen, and they were approaching her apartment complex when she came out of suspended animation. She dug the card for the gate out of her pocket and held it out to him. "Not yet." It was more bitter than she'd intended, but his statement had ripped away her filters.

Josh slipped the card from her hand and slowed to a stop in front of the gate. He swiped the card and handed it back. "I don't have any plans to start lying to you, either."

The hurt in his voice tempered her bitterness and loosened her tongue. Her hand found his neck, rested tentatively then kneaded out knots she knew her situation had tied. "I'm sorry. That didn't come out right."

"No, it didn't." He sat with his left hand tight on the steering wheel and didn't speak again until he pulled into a space in front of her building. "I'm trying not to take it personally." He surveyed the area, never once looking at her.

"It's just that—"

Josh's fingers on her wrist stopped her next words and

stilled her hand. He stared across the parking lot at the end of her building. If he paid any attention, he should be able to feel the way her pulse quickened with a blend of fear and something else she was only just beginning to admit.

He swallowed hard. "Out my window, right by the corner of your apartment. I'm pretty sure that's the truck Cameron was driving the last time we saw him."

Adrenaline hit Andrea's system so hard pain jolted through her heart. The front end of a pickup truck, bumper shining in the early morning light, peeked from a parking space around the edge of the building. She slipped out of the car and moved to stand in front of the vehicle.

Josh met her there and gripped her biceps in a way that said she wasn't going anywhere without him.

In a sane moment, she'd resent the implication that she couldn't take care of herself, but right now, it was good to have someone stronger nearby. "Are you sure it's him?"

Josh didn't release her arm. "That's the same truck. It has to be. It has the same dent in the front fender."

"Why would he call me away then show up here?" Unless the confrontation with Dutch and Mr. Miller and the arrival of the police had scared him away. He knew she'd come home eventually. The final showdown could be starting right now.

Josh's shoulder brushed hers as he stepped closer. "Get in the car and stay there." He pulled away and crept to the side of the building, edging along the brick in a way Andrea remembered from urban warfare training. Problem was, this wasn't training, and Josh entered the situation already injured, without the advantage of body armor and an M-16.

She caught him near the stairwell. "I'm going with you."

"It's too dangerous."

Andrea stepped closer. "Everything I do is dangerous right now, including waiting alone in that car." Her old training rushed forward, and she crouched lower. "I'm not letting you go without me."

He shot her a look that said this would definitely be a topic of discussion later, even though he kept silent.

Together, they crept along the warm brick until they reached the end of the building. Andrea scanned the small overflow parking lot and the trees beyond, knowing Josh did the same. Finally, he gave her a final signal for silence and slipped around the corner.

Andrea held her breath, then followed as Josh took a step back and crashed into her.

"No." The groan fell from his mouth and hit the pavement like a flat basketball.

Over his shoulder, Andrea caught a glimpse of the cab of the truck as the sun filtered through the trees and tinted the glass bright red.

Her breath caught, allowing nausea to rise in a sickening wave. She swayed on her feet.

That wasn't reflected sunlight spattering the windows.

It was blood.

Déjà vu. Or a really bad recurring nightmare. That's what all of this had to be.

Josh leaned back against the hood of a police car in front of Andrea's apartment and ran both hands through his hair, staring at the pavement between his feet. He'd lost count of how many times he'd seen emergency lights and heard wailing sirens in the past few days. If he never experienced either again, he'd die a happy man.

The tips of no-nonsense brown shoes appeared in his

line of sight. He didn't have to look up to know who'd be staring him down. He'd been waiting for her.

In an oddly out of character gesture, Detective Simmons hesitated before she leaned against the hood of the car about a foot away from him. She gave him a hard look, then turned her gaze to a third-floor window where Andrea looked down at them, once again wrapped in a blanket. If Josh hadn't caught her shoulder earlier, she'd have rocked backward and smacked the brick corner of her building with the back of her head. Even now, she seemed fragile and wounded, like she might have endured one blow too many.

The detective brushed invisible lint from the knee of her khaki pants. "After the week she's had, I'm surprised she's not in shock."

Josh hazarded another glance at the detective, but she was watching Andrea. "You're not going to accuse her of something this morning, are you?" His stiff fingers gingerly kneaded the tight muscles above his elbow. "Murder, maybe?"

A ghost of a smile crossed the woman's face, and Josh realized she was younger than he'd originally judged. She tapped the badge hanging around her neck. "I'm the good guy, remember?"

Josh straightened his arm, pulling tight muscles, and tried to assume an air of calm for Andrea who, even from this distance, still seemed deathly pale.

"And no. I'm not going to accuse her of anything. Guy in the apartment across from hers said he heard a vehicle backfire around five this morning. Since most engines don't exactly backfire nowadays, my guess is he heard something else. No—" she tugged on her badge "—your Miss Donovan is in the clear."

"But I'm not." With glittering clarity, Josh knew why she'd settled beside him.

"Nobody said that." Her voice was practiced and even.

"Mmm-hmm." He kept his eyes pinned on Andrea. "I'll go ahead and tell you I was home all night until I came here. Wide awake and hopped up on adrenaline and ibuprofen. And nobody else was with me."

Detective Simmons chuckled. "You're safe, Walker."

He turned wary eyes to her. "That was too easy."

"You were with her at the time of death." She glanced at him for his reaction then looked back at the building in front of them when he didn't give one. "The apartment complex's gate camera caught Cameron's vehicle entering by tailgating another vehicle going through the security gate. It was after you two left." The car rocked slightly as she shifted position. "We still need to talk about why you decided to do something as foolish as sneaking off to her office in the dark. What were you after?"

Josh needed to avoid the coming lecture. If she chastised him for trying to protect his soldier or Andrea, there was no way his anger would stay below the surface. "What about Dutch?"

"I can't comment on that yet. Only thing I can say is it's a good thing we had eyes on the building. And Dutch had nothing to do with this shooting, not based on when we believe it happened. Even if he is your guy, he's only one of several, based on the look of things."

That's what he'd been most afraid of. This was bigger than it seemed, with too many threads tangling around each other. If only they could find the one string that unraveled everything, before anyone else got killed. "Is that really Cameron in the truck?"

"We're pretty sure it is."

Josh's eyes narrowed, his mind desperate to grasp anything other than the emotion that tried to rush him. "*Pretty sure?* How could you not be..." Nausea made him grip the hood of the car so hard the metal dug into his fingers.

"Yeah." The detective's voice was laced with the slightest tinge of disgust. "High powered, high caliber to the back of the head. Small hole on the back side..."

"Massive destruction on the front side." Josh couldn't stop the film rolling in his head. Only once had he seen what that kind of power could do on exit, and the sight had been one that still woke him in a cold sweat. Now Cameron was gone, his physical self obliterated by an unseen enemy.

"We'll have to wait on a positive ID, but preliminary evidence suggests it's him."

Reality broke through to hit Josh like Andrea's unexpected right hook had a few days ago. He'd lost a couple of guys in Afghanistan and Iraq. Though tragic, it wasn't the same kind of shock this was. This hit like lightning, unexpected and out of place.

Then the voice started an unending loop. Another person in his shadow dead. Another person he'd failed to protect. The names played like roll call: Lauren, Brendan, Cameron... *Please don't let Andrea be next.*

He kicked a wayward pebble across the pavement and forced his mind onto a different path.

"You know..." From the sound of the detective's voice, he could tell she'd turned away from him. "This isn't your fault."

His head snapped up like her words had him on a leash. Had she read his mind?

She looked back at him so fast he didn't have a chance to turn away. For a minute, she didn't say anything, then she let her attention go back to the reflected lights of the emergency vehicles behind them. "You'll figure that out eventually."

It was too soon since his own realization. This was a subject he didn't want to get into now, and certainly not with a woman he hardly knew and wasn't even sure he liked.

Detective Simmons didn't give him a chance to think, anyway. "You did a pretty good job at deflecting me earlier, but I haven't forgotten. Do you want to tell me what you two were doing at the counseling center? Like I said, there's no Waffle House nearby, so you weren't headed out for breakfast."

"Be nice if life were that simple." He kept his eyes on Andrea, who talked with a man he assumed was another detective while a paramedic stood at her side holding a blood pressure cuff. "Cameron called and said he was ready to talk, that he'd meet us there."

"And here I thought you were smarter than that." Her shoes scraped softly on the pavement as she moved slightly away from him.

Smarter than that? He'd like to cop an attitude and tell her she couldn't imply he was stupid, but the raw truth was he'd known all along he was juggling danger like a hand grenade with the pin pulled.

"If I had to guess, I'd say Wade Cameron knew you guys are being watched by whoever is after him. Smart move, calling the two of you away. Anybody watching would follow you, leaving him free to come here. The question is why." She leaned her head back and squinted against the bright light of morning. "Either that or you're being set up."

"Set up?" Josh pulled his gaze from Andrea and tried to gauge the emotion behind the detective's words. "You know we didn't do this. So you're clearing Andrea of everything?"

"Yet another thing I didn't say. I'll be honest with you, Walker. To my thinking, this isn't about Wade Cameron. Yes, he's dead. But every single incident aside from this one has been directly aimed at Andrea Donovan. Either somebody thinks she knows something, or she's knee-deep in everything that's going on and somebody wants her quiet."

"They want her to shut down. And they think she knows something." He knew Andrea, knew how much she loved her brother and how that love extended to every person who suffered from PTSD and addiction like he did. He would lay his life down on the belief that she was innocent. "If somebody killed Cameron, it's because they're cleaning house and running scared. They'll take care of anyone who could point fingers at them."

"Already floated that theory. Off the record, it's my favorite."

For the first time, Josh believed Detective Simmons had a heart and that it was on Andrea's side. "Did you tell her that's Cameron in the truck?"

"No." She turned to walk away but looked back at Josh over her shoulder as she did. "I told *you*."

Even though she hadn't said it, Josh knew her implication was right. Andrea would take the news better from him. He ran his hand down his face and along his chin, wondering when the last time was he'd let a razor hit his face. The last day he'd worked. Whenever that had been. Right now, it felt like two lifetimes ago.

Josh braced his hands on the car behind him to push up, but his right elbow collapsed under the pressure and set him back hard against the vehicle. To be perfectly honest, he was tired of being mocked and reminded of his weakness every time he moved.

He heaved himself up and put one foot in front of the other as Andrea looked down and met his gaze.

A reverberating crack split the air. A shout echoed off the trees as the glass between them shattered and Andrea slipped from view.

FOURTEEN

Blood. Andrea stared at her fingers as strong hands yanked her up and pulled her across the carpet into her kitchen against the cabinet.

Josh. Where was Josh?

Shouts and pounding feet ebbed and flowed around her as hands gripped her face and turned her head, forcing her to meet the concerned eyes of the paramedic she'd chatted with moments before. He scanned her face then shifted out of her line of vision. Wet warmth trickled its way down her temple to her cheek, but her arms felt too heavy to lift them and swipe it away.

Someone slid into place beside her. "Andrea, look at me. Did they hit you?"

Breath entered her lungs all at once, and she realized she'd held it until that moment, waiting for him. Josh knelt beside her, pale and breathing hard. "You okay?" Her words felt and sounded like cold molasses.

"I'm fine." He stretched a hand toward her forehead then stopped and let it hover between them. "You're bleeding."

The young paramedic reappeared, his hands sheathed in disposable gloves. He pressed a stinging compress to her temple. "I think she got hit by glass from the window. I don't see anything else, no other wounds." His voice shook slightly as he checked beneath the compress and pressed more firmly. "We should have had you away from that window. Letting you stand there with all that's happened wasn't smart."

"Everybody's okay?" Josh was fine, here beside her as always, but Andrea needed to know, needed assurance that no one else suffered because of her. Enough was enough. All she wanted to do was shove the paramedic aside and march into the center of the parking lot with her hands over her head. When bravado had led her to tell Josh they'd never shut her down, nobody had died, no other shots had been fired. But now someone was dead. She had to find the way to end this. Now.

"Fine, as far as I know." The young paramedic taped a bandage over the wound, handed her a stack of wet wipes, then vanished from her narrow field of vision. It was like she couldn't get her head on straight, like she was swimming through maple syrup.

"There was only the one shot." Josh took the packets from her hands and ripped two open, then started gently wiping her blood from her fingers.

Her blood. How close had she come to being hit this time? She wanted to verbalize the question, but the words stuck between her head and her tongue. All she could do was sit mute and watch Josh's fingers on hers.

Gradually, her body calmed, but everything focused with laser precision on the warmth of Josh's fingers. That seemed to be the center, the thing that pulled her into reality and knocked back the shock of gunshots and flying glass. She drew in a shaky breath but didn't look up. "Was that Wade? In the truck?" It had gnawed at her since they backed away and called the police, taking refuge in her apartment.

Josh ripped open another wipe. "You got a carpet burn on your palm." He reached for her other hand and turned it over. "This one, too."

"Josh." She tried to pull away from the electricity his hand conducted even in the middle of chaos, but his grip tightened. "It was him, wasn't it? And then they waited for me." The words choked on the edge of sobs. The answer was the last thing she wanted to hear, even though she already knew it.

Josh's fingers stilled. Slowly, as though he felt her need to know that she was still alive, that he was still alive, even in the face of a brutal murder, he lifted her hand and pressed a kiss to her palm. Then he raised his eyes and they focused straight in on hers. His grip on her fingers tightened, and he reached up with his free hand to brush the hair from her bandage, then found her eyes again.

The rest of the chaos faded away. They were already alone in her kitchen, but the shouts from outside and the police radios died away until the only sound was their breathing. The tiny voice that told her Josh was in danger if she let him get any closer grew more and more distant as he let his fingers trail down her face, his eyes asking for permission she shouldn't give but couldn't stop herself from granting.

With a deep inhale Josh leaned forward and pressed his lips beside the bandage on her forehead.

Unwanted disappointment coursed through Andrea. Even though she knew they didn't need the distraction now, she'd wanted him to kiss her with everything in her being.

Now was not the time. It would be wrong, when Wade's body lay downstairs, when grief threatened to shred the last ounce of her sanity. She slid closer to Josh and buried her face in the solid wall of his chest. Andrea willed herself not to cry, but when his arm slipped around her and he whispered, "It's okay," all of the barriers holding back her tears failed.

Her muscles melted along with her emotions, sagging her against him. Josh's arms tightened around her, his chin resting on her head, snuggling her deeper against the hollow of his throat. In that quiet haven, she poured out the shock of Wade Cameron's death, though in her mind, he had her brother's face. Grief over Brendan and Wade melted together and erupted in a storm of tears and sobs that should have scared Josh straight into the next county. Instead, he held her closer.

As her tears ebbed, a new resolve crept in. She needed Josh. There was no denying it now. In spite of days and years worth of pain, the emotion refused to be beaten back.

But saying that to him now was only asking for trouble for both of them.

Andrea gently pushed away and swept her hair from her forehead, then wiped her eyes. She brushed off her shirt, then moved to stand. She had to get out of here, away from him, away from anybody else who could be caught in the crossfire. When this was over, then she could look him in the eye and tell him how deep her feelings ran.

Josh reached out and caught her wrist, wrecking her balance and settling her right back to the floor. "Where do you think you're going?"

"Out. To make sure everyone's okay."

He shook his head and released her hand to brush a stray tendril behind her ear. "I can't let you go out there. That shot was aimed straight at you, and there's no telling whether or not the shooter is still waiting. The police are clearing the area. Give them time before you paint a bull's-eye on your forehead and walk through that door."

In the living room, the blinds clicked in the warm breeze of an ironically perfect July morning. “You’re safe in here. Don’t make me hog-tie you to a chair, because I will if it will keep you alive.”

Andrea eyed him. She ought to defy him and march right out that door, but he was right. At least in the windowless kitchen, the shooter couldn’t get a bead on her. They played visual chicken for a moment before she settled back against him. “Why do you think they want me to shut down? Why listen in on my sessions? How does this all tie in to Wade?”

Josh hesitated, then slipped an arm around her and drew her head to his shoulder. “They’re pretty sure that was him in the truck.”

“What do you mean by that? Can’t they just look at him and tell?” It hadn’t dawned on her till now that Josh had never really answered her question about Wade.

Josh shook his head, and cold realization ran down Andrea’s spine. Her life was officially the worst horror story ever written. Thugs and bullets and men without faces, theoretically and actually.

She fought back tears. Crying was getting old. Trembling was getting old. Fear was getting old. “Well, I’m no good to anybody dead.” She shook her head and nestled deeper into his shoulder, willing to believe the lie that she was safe right here.

“Something doesn’t make sense.” Josh squeezed her closer. “Why not take the shot when you were in the open, close to Cameron’s truck? Why wait all this time for the police to show up then aim through a partially covered window?” The last word trailed off, as though swallowed by a thought Andrea couldn’t follow. He slipped his arm from her shoulder and looked down at her. “They aren’t trying to kill you.”

"So bullets are the new way to say 'I can be your friend?'"

"You hide behind that sarcasm when you're scared."

Her mouth opened, but the planned denial didn't come.

"If they wanted you dead," Josh went on like he hadn't just laid a finger on her emotional pulse, "you'd be dead. In front of the PX two days ago."

"They tried to hit me with a car."

He nodded. "I watched it play out. The driver swerved away from the direction you jumped. And yesterday, at the church, they gave us time to see them before they opened fire. I'd already pulled you out of the way when the bullets started flying."

Andrea squeezed her eyes shut, blocking out the too-bright room. "You're not making any sense." Maybe she was woozier than she'd originally thought. Maybe the shock of flying glass and blood and bullets had dragged her into a panic attack that completely wiped out reality, but Josh's words didn't compute. "Why go to all this trouble if they don't want me dead?"

"Because of what you just said. You're no good to them dead, but for some reason they want you scared."

Andrea pulled away from Josh and stood, pacing her kitchen. She felt exposed, even in this windowless room with policemen outside her door. She picked up a spoon rest and let the cool weight press against her palm. "Scared of what?" Metal clanged against granite as she slammed it to the counter. The utensils in the drawer beneath jumped and rattled.

"Nothing else makes sense."

"Nothing at all makes sense." She leaned against the counter and stared at the front of the refrigerator, where a picture of her and her parents at graduation hung beneath a magnet. The urge to rip it from the door and tear it into pieces made her fingers ache. How good a therapist was she when the client she was most proud of dove into this kind of ridiculous situation and got himself killed?

"These are people who aren't thinking rationally. But think about it. Now is the perfect time to come at you. Your parents are on vacation. Grace is out of town, too. You're alone." He opened and shut two cabinet doors, as if he was taking out his frustration on the wood. "They just didn't count on me showing up."

Andrea's head couldn't take the banging anymore. "What are you doing?"

"Where are your glasses?" He stopped and looked over his shoulder at her. "You need water or something. You're still shaking."

Balling her fingers into fists to stop the tremors she hadn't realized were so obvious, Andrea nodded toward the cabinet beside the sink. "Up there." She wrapped her arms around herself. "So what do I do? How do I make this stop?"

The silence drew tight, and Andrea looked up at Josh.

He stared into her cabinet at her coffee mugs. "I think we just got one step closer to our answer."

Josh lifted a finger toward the back wall of the cabinet then stopped, mindful of the dangers of contaminating the evidence. There, scrawled across the wood in the same red marker as the hidden message from the wall locker were the numbers *00 12 30.*

Andrea studied the writing. They'd been staring at it for the past two minutes, but so far she hadn't said one word. She looked tense, as if the ink were a coiled rattlesnake that could strike at any moment.

"Andrea, do you have your phone? I left mine in the car."

She pulled her phone from her pocket and automatically snapped a picture of the numbers before slipping the phone back into place.

"Could you take a picture of it?" Josh bumped her shoulder with his. He was trying to draw a smile, a chuckle, from her, anything but the silent stoicism that had her locked inside herself. When she didn't respond, he scanned her profile. Nearly colorless lips pulled tight against her teeth. He contemplated having the paramedic check for shock again when her voice interrupted his thoughts.

"Will you stop staring at me?" She didn't look away from the cabinet in front of her, though the corner of her mouth tipped up. "You're wrecking my focus."

"What focus? I thought you'd gone out of your head."

She nodded toward the writing. "I know I've seen this someplace before. It's just not kicking in. There's an emotional memory tied to it, but it doesn't make any sense."

Josh turned and leaned back against the counter so he could be free to watch her face as she puzzled out the riddle. "What is it you're remembering?"

Her eyes flicked to him and back to the cabinet as an embarrassed little blush pinked her cheeks. "Gym socks."

Josh drew his head back and suppressed a smile. "Gym socks are not an emotion, Donovan."

"I know. But it's almost carefree and happy to me. For some reason, when I look at this I see and feel—"

"Sweat?"

"Not helping."

"Well, neither is gym socks. Although I could go for a long workout to clear my head if they ever let us out of here." Josh couldn't stop himself. He ran a hand down her hair and tucked a lock of it behind her ear, pulling back the curtain that shaded her face.

She didn't spare him a glance. "How did it get here? It sure wasn't there when I came home last night, and trust me, nobody came through that door before you got here."

"It had to be while we were on our wild goose chase at your office." The detective's earlier comments whispered against the edges of his thoughts. "This wasn't a setup. It was a chance for Cameron to communicate with you. He's trying to tell you something."

"Why me?" She tipped her head back, and Josh had to look away from the curve of her neck. After a second of looking for answers in the popcorn ceiling, she sighed. "We have to tell Detective Simmons. See if she can figure it out."

"That's a different tune than you were singing earlier."

"Yeah, well, that was before somebody died and I nearly got killed. Again." Her eyes hooded, like she was about to retreat. If this kept up, he might lose her forever to that dark room that fed off the fear in her heart.

Josh slapped his hands together, jolting Andrea nearly out of her skin. "Before we do, let's go with that whole gym socks thing. Whaddaya say? I can psychoanalyze you this time." He jerked a thumb over his shoulder. "Want to go in the den so you can lay on the couch? Every time I dreamed of being a psychologist, I dreamed I had a couch."

"You never dreamed of being a psychologist. You majored in sports medicine."

His eyebrow arched high, pulling at the bruise on his cheek. "And you know this how?"

There went that pink blush again. "Maybe your mom told my mom."

"Mmm-hmm." While that was a path he'd like to meander down, there wasn't much time before someone came in and caught them with the latest evidence. With the dressing down he'd received from Detective Simmons earlier, if they were busted again it wouldn't go easy. "So, smelly...dirty..." He rolled his hand as if asking her for more images.

Andrea swallowed hard and squeezed her eyebrows together. "Gym clothes...lockers..." She stopped breathing. Excitement widened her eyes. "High school. Our gym lockers had combination locks. Mine started with a double zero." She gripped Josh's right biceps and he tried not to wince as the motion jerked at his elbow. "Just like that one." Yanking her hands from his arm, she fluttered them in front of her face as though the action would make the memories come faster. "That's a combination to a lock." She reached into her pocket and yanked out her phone, scrolling through the screens. "And locks lock lockers—"

"Or storage units." Josh straightened and gestured to her phone. "That other message was a storage unit, wasn't it?"

A tap on the door frame ended their furtive guesses. Andrea slipped her phone into her pocket as they turned.

Detective Simmons stood in the kitchen entry. "You guys look as guilty as two kids playing hooky on the first day of senior year."

Josh arched an eyebrow. The woman was growing on him, becoming more of an ally every second. "I think we found something."

"Where and when? You haven't left this apartment since that shot was fired."

Josh waved her closer, then shifted to make room for her at the cabinet. "Y'all find the shooter?"

Detective Simmons's steps across the white linoleum were as measured as her demeanor. "No. But we found where he holed up—in the tree line on the other side of the parking lot. The angle he had on this place would have allowed him to hit Cameron and still hit that window. But I'm going to tell you..." Her gaze pegged Andrea. "He's a crack shot to have hit Cameron from that angle and at that distance. He missed you on purpose."

Josh met her eyes over the detective's shoulder. Just like he'd said. "They're out to scare her."

"That'd be my guess." Detective Simmons focused on the red scrawl. "How did you find that?"

"Looking for a glass," Josh replied.

"Either of you touch it?"

Josh shook his head and aimed a finger at the front edge of the door. "Just that part there, when I pulled it open. I wasn't sure what you needed to check, so I was careful."

She shot him an impressed glance. "Ever thought of being a cop when you retire?"

"I don't plan to retire."

"Old soldiers never die," she muttered. "I'd say nice work, but that would make me sound like a TV cop, wouldn't it?" She removed gloves from her pocket and pulled them on with a snap. "I'll get someone in here to photograph it. You two have any more theories to pitch?"

Before either of them could say anything, a uniformed officer appeared at the door. "We found something."

Simmons nodded and headed for the door. "You two clear out. You can't hang around until we've gone through this place. Just stay low." She left before either of them could say anything.

Andrea's shoulders slumped. "My apartment is a crime scene. My office is a crime scene. I've got nowhere to go."

"One thing at a time." He tugged at her hand, desperate to shake her out of what was certain to be a spiral into shock. "Simmons said the words. We're free to go. Anywhere you want."

"Anywhere out of rifle range." The fight inside her played out across her face. The instant she won, it was obvious in her expression. Her eyes opened. "Maybe I just need food." Andrea grabbed her keys from the counter and shoved them into her pocket, then glanced around. "Somewhere without windows."

Josh watched her and wondered how much longer this would go on. His four-day weekend ended tomorrow. She'd planned to reopen the counseling center. Time to protect her was running out.

Someone cleared his throat and jerked their attention to the door. The man Andrea had been talking with at the church yesterday stood watching them. He stepped up and extended a hand to Josh. "Detective Martin."

"Josh Walker."

The detective's grip was steady, his eyes serious. "Detective Simmons had a few questions for you about what you found up here."

Josh nodded, though his stomach protested so loudly, he knew everyone heard it. Now that things had calmed down, all he could think about was food.

Detective Martin arched an eyebrow.

Andrea whacked Josh in the abs with the back of her hand. "Leave it to you to start thinking with your stomach."

He rubbed the spot like she'd wounded him. "What can I say? Near-death experiences make me ravenous."

"Then I should be dead of starvation."

As Josh started to walk away, Andrea moved to follow him, but Detective Martin held up a hand. "I've got a couple guys going over to the center to check out a few things, but I assume your office is locked."

"If you want, I can give you the key. How's that?" Andrea pulled the key ring from her pocket.

"Perfect."

Josh waited as she twisted the key off, but she waved him away. "Don't just stand there, Walker. Women and children are starving. Go answer her questions."

"You sure?"

She leveled a gaze on him like his mother used to do when he wasn't moving fast enough to stow his ball glove and mow the lawn.

He flipped a salute and was halfway down the stairs when she called, "And see if she can arrange an armored car for us."

Josh chuckled and descended the stairs, scanning the apartment's parking lot. A uniformed officer stood on the sidewalk, and Josh stopped. "You know where Detective Simmons went?"

The man pointed toward the trees, where Detective Simmons was heading toward the wood line, crossing the small lawn. Josh jogged across the parking lot and caught her as she reached the trees.

She tipped her head to the side. "Think of something else, First Sergeant?"

"Detective Martin said you wanted to ask me a few more questions."

Her expression hardened before she shook her head. "I'm the only detective here. We don't have a Detective Martin."

FIFTEEN

Detective Martin watched Josh leave, then turned to Andrea. He let her fiddle with the key ring for a second, then glanced at his watch. "Would you mind walking out with me while you wrestle that thing? They've put me on a timeline. Sooner I get over there and back, the better."

She shrugged. "No problem."

He stepped through the door onto the cement walkway ahead of her, glancing both ways, then motioned her forward. "Heard you found another piece of Cameron's puzzle."

Andrea nodded, abandoning her keys as she navigated the steep steps. "Detective Simmons is working on it. And we think we've figured out what it is." She grunted as her forehead crashed into the shoulder of the detective, who had stopped dead at the foot of the stairs.

He stood there, his eyes on the parking lot, then grabbed her by the upper arm and dragged her toward the thin stretch of asphalt. "You figured it out?"

Her feet tripping under her, Andrea skidded along behind the detective and tried to jerk her arm away. "A storage unit. But—" she yanked again "—what are you doing?"

The midsummer blast of air when they stepped into

the sunlight was heavy and warm. Andrea had a tough time taking in a satisfying breath.

"We're going to where you can tell me what you know."

The ambulance Andrea had seen pull in earlier was backed up to the sidewalk. Before she could protest, Detective Martin shoved her inside, climbed in after her and yanked the door shut. "Go. Now." His voice rang deep and angry.

The ambulance lurched forward, and Andrea turned back to the man in front of her.

He studied her with eyes that glittered hard, and reality crashed in. She was in a wide-awake nightmare with no way out. She wanted to scream, wanted to run, wanted to do something, but no sound or movement would come. The moment she opened her mouth, the man who called himself Detective Martin was on her, his hand blocking any sound.

God, help me.

"Don't," he ground out through gritted teeth. "You're only alive now because you're the only person who holds the information we need, but don't think I'll hesitate to shut you up by any means necessary." His fingers pinched her skin so tight she could feel bruises rising.

He pinned her to the seat until the ambulance picked up speed and Andrea knew they were on the main road. Once they were a safe distance from her apartment, Martin backed away. He pulled a pistol from his pocket and braced it on the seat beside him, not physically threatening her, but letting her know without words that she dare not try anything.

She drew in a welcome breath and eyed the oxygen tank, wishing for a jolt of pure air but surprised at the deep calm she felt. Her heart raced triple time, but her mind dragged slower, methodically thinking through every option. From here, there was nothing she could do. Her goal was to stay alive until someone figured out she was gone and came after her.

But who knew how long that would take?

Andrea squared her shoulders, bound and determined to show her attacker he didn't scare her, even though her pulse rate said otherwise. "You're no detective."

"Very good." He tipped his head toward the front of the vehicle.

"How did you get so close to me? Yesterday, you were at the church. And today..."

He shrugged. "When you're there before the area's taped off, it's easy to blend in. When I started asking you questions and dropped the right names, you made a lot of stupid assumptions about who I am. And everyone who saw me talking to you assumed I was someone you knew. It wasn't that hard. I just stayed out of your detective's way." He leaned forward, false compassion burning in his eyes. "Next time someone tells you they're a cop, you should ask to see a badge." He sat back and patted his pockets with his free hand. "Seems I left mine at home."

Stupid. She and Josh had done a lot of dumb things the past few days, but not asking to see ID on the man questioning her was the worst.

"Don't beat yourself up too much. We've been doing this a long time in a lot of places. You're an amateur up against pros. It was only a matter of time before you stumbled." The man leaned forward so that his face was inches from hers. "Now. Tell me what you figured out. You can start with that last piece of information First Sergeant Walker found."

Andrea shook her head and backed as far as she could against the wall, digging her voice up from where it had plummeted to her toes. "I do that, and you'll kill me right here."

He sat back and tapped his finger on the gun, still flat on the seat beside him. "I think we've already proven more than once we're not out to kill you. We don't need your blood on our hands."

"You're lying. You killed Wade, so there's no reason you wouldn't take me out next."

His eyebrow arched as he tipped his head to the side. "You're way too smart to have fallen for something as stupid as me being a cop." He chuckled. "You're right. But look at it this way. Either way you're dead. At least make it mean something."

"You're out of luck. Without all of the pieces, you don't have enough information to locate and access."

She sat back, arms crossed, allowing a look of triumph to creep onto her face. He could kill her if he wanted, but he wasn't going to get a thing out of her for the trouble.

"Check her cell phone." The voice came from the front of the ambulance.

For the first time, Andrea considered the driver.

It was the young paramedic who had worked on her earlier. He'd been in and out of the apartment the entire time she and Josh talked, practically invisible to her.

Her jaw fell open before she could stop it.

The fake detective chuckled low. "See, Ms. Donovan? You just can't win." He held out his hand, palm up. "Now you can hand your phone over, or I can take it by force."

Andrea considered her options. There was nowhere to run in the crowded back of the ambulance, and he definitely had the size advantage, not to mention the gun.

Conceding to temporary defeat, she passed the phone to him as the ambulance slowed.

Martin flicked through, then pulled out his own cell

phone and pressed the screen. "Yeah. It's me. If I'm deciphering this right, it's the storage place at 5977 Whitesville Road. You were right about it being this side of town." He flipped through her phone again. "Looks like the unit you're looking for is D-4 and the combination is probably 00-12-30."

And just like that, the men who'd pursued her knew everything. As the ambulance made a gentle turn, she swayed with it, helplessness weighing her.

They were hardly stopped before the doors swung open to reveal two men, guns trained on them. For one heartbeat, Andrea sagged in relief. She was safe.

But then the barrels turned to her and she knew… There was no way she was getting out of this alive.

By the time Josh yanked open the door to the apartment, his lungs were near exploding. A shot of cool air burned in his chest, and it was a moment before he could call out for her. "Andrea!"

Nothing. The only movement in the entire room was the window blind swaying in the breeze.

He was in the middle of the kitchen when Detective Simmons and two other officers bolted through the doors. "They here?"

Josh aimed a finger at the hallway, the habit of command driving him to take charge, to do something. "Check the rest of the place." He hoped against every negative thought in him that this Martin character had locked her in her bedroom and hadn't somehow managed to make off with her right under everyone's noses.

The kitchen and den looked no different than when he'd left a couple of minutes before. He spun back into the hallway in time to catch Detective Simmons's curt head shake.

Andrea and the fake detective couldn't have disappeared into vapor. He gripped the back of his neck. Then again, Cameron had done the same thing to him just a few days ago. Vanished, evaporated. He rolled his eyes heavenward. Only this time, there was no way they'd crawled through the ceiling.

"Has anyone left the scene?" One of the uniforms near Simmons spoke into his radio and waited for an answer.

The squawk came immediately. "Just the ambulance. About five minutes ago."

Josh's stomach seemed to hit the soles of his running shoes. The ambulance. The one he'd stepped aside to let pass in the parking lot as he made the mad dash back to the building with the officers on his tail.

Detective Simmons's mouth drew into a grim line. She snatched the radio from the officer's hand. "Track down that ambulance. Now. Our suspects have Andrea Donovan in it." She smacked the radio against the officer's chest and stalked across the room to Josh. "We will find her."

She was gone with the other officers before he could respond, leaving him alone to kick himself in the teeth. He sank onto the same ottoman where he'd comforted Andrea two days before. This was it. This time there was no denying his culpability. He'd killed her.

No. Even as he thought it, he shot to his feet. There was no way he'd give up, not until he had her back. Not until every last option died in front of his eyes. This was different than staring helplessly at charred wreckage. This time, there was hope.

The danger hadn't fully seeped in when Martin stepped down from the ambulance then reached up and, ironically, helped Andrea to the ground. She was shuffled into the backseat of a white SUV and seated between the new guys with guns before she could get her bearings. By the time her trouble sank in all the way and she figured out they were in the parking lot of her church, the ambulance and Martin were gone.

"Well, Ms. Andrea. Here we are." A familiar voice drifted from the front seat, washing relief over the fear and ebbing the tension from her muscles.

Safe! She was safe. Only... She still sat here between two armed men. A wave of relief crested on panicked uncertainty. As strange as everything had been up until now, this really felt like her sanity was gone. "Mr. Miller?"

The man turned from the front passenger seat, his round face hard behind eyes that glittered. "You should have listened early on. Then we wouldn't be where we are now."

This was not the man who daily brought her coffee. Who smiled and laughed and teased her about whom she should marry someday. This was a man with a jaw set into a hard line by contempt. "I'm not... I don't..." Her thoughts wouldn't form; the words couldn't come. The world felt as if it were spinning out of control. Seeking a solid place, her fingers sought the edge of the seat, but grasped the knee of the giant beside her instead.

He laughed.

Jerking her hand back, she clasped her hands between her knees so tightly her fingertips went numb. "I don't understand."

"What is there to understand? When you moved into the building, I first thought having you near would be a nuisance, at best. But then I realized the easy pickings of a rehab clinic right next door. So I tried a little experiment with Mr. Cameron. As it turns out, it doesn't take much to tempt a man back into old habits."

An experiment? On Wade? Why would it matter to

Mr. Miller whether or not Wade stayed clean and sober? Unless… The SUV seemed to wobble beneath her, and she clasped her palms tighter together, biting the inside of her lip.

One of the gunmen shifted away from her. "If she loses her breakfast, I'm shooting her."

"Weak stomach, Taylor?" Mr. Miller shook his head. "Never would have thought that of you."

"You know better. I got new shoes."

It was too bad the nausea waned as the seconds ticked away. Ruining expensive leather might have been fitting payback, even if it did get her killed. Still, it took a minute for her jaw to ease so she could speak. "You're the reason Wade relapsed? You're the one selling drugs? You're the reason I was under surveillance by the cops?" Anger rose and squashed fear. Every accusation that had been leveled at her had come from this man, who had pretended to be her friend so he could keep an eye on her patients, on her. "You listened in on my sessions to find my patients' weaknesses and turn them into your customers?"

"Just Cameron so far. We were just getting started."

The betrayal didn't fuel the fire half so much as his callous indifference toward Wade. "You ruined his life."

"Good thing it was a short life."

Andrea lunged at him, her shoulders nearly clearing the front seat before one of the guards grabbed her hair and yanked her back, shooting fire through her scalp. Tears clawed at her eyes, but she refused to let them come. These men weren't dealing with a weak-kneed crybaby who'd back down just because they threatened her. If they wanted something from her, they'd have to fight for it. In spite of the pain, she prepared to lunge again, but a corded forearm pressed against her neck, forcing her back in the seat.

She breathed hard and forced her muscles to relax. There were too many questions, and if these men planned to kill her, she planned to make them talk as much as possible before they did. "Why try to shut me down?"

"You started talking to the cops. Your little operation was more liability than profit maker at that moment. You should have taken off like we asked you to."

"Asked? Or bullied?"

He shrugged, bouncing slightly as the driver pressed the gas and tore them out of the parking lot toward Veterans Parkway.

"I started talking to the police because your *friend* tried to kidnap me."

"Nice try. You've been watching us and feeding information to your fake homeless friend for quite some time, have you not?"

"What? Dutch?" Again, everything made less and less sense. "He's a homeless vet who empties my trash."

"He's a detective."

"What?" The word would have been a whisper even if the giant beside her hadn't pressed harder on her windpipe. All of those missing puzzle pieces clicked into place. Dutch's near-constant presence. His questions. The gun. He'd been watching her all along, likely seeing her friendship with the gas station owner as convicting evidence.

Somehow, Dutch's true identity hurt worse than that of the man in front of her. Her chest ached. Nobody was who they seemed to be.

Except Josh.

"Don't pretend you didn't know." Mr. Miller drew his head back and arched an eyebrow, flicking a glance at the men on either side of her. "That's the first move in every informant's playbook."

"I didn't." She hated the way her voice pleaded like a

teenager, whining about how unfair life is. Ironic, since it was likely Andrea was pleading for her own life.

"Nice try. You befriended me way too easily."

"I could say the same of you and your daily coffee deliveries."

With satisfaction, Andrea watched something like frustration flash on his face. They'd expected her to back down, to knuckle under quietly and give them everything they wanted. She refused. Something told her this belief she knew something was the only thing keeping her alive, and if she had to play coy with them to survive, she'd do it to the last ounce of her strength.

Beside her, the two men tensed as the atmosphere in the car changed. Apparently, this attitude was something nobody saw coming.

Good. Maybe this was her salvation. If she had information they needed, they wouldn't kill her. And there had to be some soft spot for her in her former "friend." He'd been much too kind to turn on her completely. The longer he stalled about killing her, the more time there was for Josh to find them, and she had no doubt he'd find her. If nothing else, he could have the cops track her location through her cell phone, which Miller still held. She had hope.

It was the ring of Miller's cell that distracted his gaze from her. He jerked the phone to his ear. "What?" As his mouth settled into a grim line, he nodded. "You took him out on Weaver Road? Good. One less bit of hush money to pay out. Head over to this address. If the cops show up, take out our guys first." He rattled off the address to the storage facility and killed the call.

Andrea controlled her breathing. "Just like that? You'd kill your own men just like that?"

"I'd rather sacrifice them than risk them talking if they're taken into custody."

The swift coldness of the statement snuffed Andrea's last hope for compassion. Anyone willing to kill his own people would never let her live.

The car slowed to a stop at Veterans and J.R. Allen, preparing to make a left onto the highway. Beside them, a high school kid with his windows down bobbed his head to the thumping rhythm from his speakers. If she could just gather enough leverage to get to the door…

The man to her left shifted. "Boss."

It only took a quick survey for Miller to read her intentions. "If you try it, I won't have them shoot you. I'll have them shoot the kid."

Their guns reappeared, both aimed at the boy in the next car. An innocent life with no clue that death was mere feet away.

Her muscles robbed of strength, Andrea sank against the leather seat.

"Wise choice." Miller nodded, and the men lowered their weapons again. "Wouldn't want someone else to die in your name, would you? Because you know, Wade Cameron stole those drugs to protect you."

Her head jerked up. "What?"

"He caught wind of the fact we'd tapped your office to mark the easy targets and that we found out you've been working with Dutch. He took out an insurance policy to protect you. Stole a mighty large stash he'd agreed to deliver. Said he'd only return it if we backed off and left you alone."

When Andrea gasped, the men beside her chuckled. Wade had died protecting her. He'd tried to warn her and she'd suspected him, tried to save her and she'd turned her back to what he was saying. If only she'd bucked Josh that night and let Wade talk in the lobby. All of this might have been prevented.

Josh. By now he was bound to have noticed she was missing. Their head start hadn't been that large. Right now he was probably planning a rescue.

"I have to hand it to the kid, though. He's one of the few people who has ever played me. He robbed us clean, hid our stuff from us and tried to extort us." Miller shrugged. "He should have known you don't mess with the big guns."

"I guess that's you?"

"Hide behind that tough front all you want, Ms. Andrea. You're not fooling me." Then he did the unthinkable. He popped the battery out of her phone and dropped it onto the floorboard, stomping the screen into fractured pieces. "Wouldn't want them to track you the same way we have."

With that possibility shattered, she was down to only one. It was a slim hope, but it was all that she had. If Josh could get to the storage unit ahead of them, he'd save her. *Please, God, show them where I am.*

Andrea's apartment parking lot filled rapidly with more people than Josh could count. He stood at the fringes, listening, knowing he shouldn't be a part of this little powwow and hoping against hope that no one noticed he was there.

"I think you're right." Detective Simmons tapped something on the hood of a vehicle. "That's Whitesville Road. It's a self-storage place."

Someone's cell phone rang and silenced the conversation.

Every nerve snapped to attention, but Josh knew none of them could match his readiness. Just tell him where to go. He'd crawl if he had to.

An officer braced a hand to Josh's chest, and he realized he was leaning forward far enough to pitch onto his face, as though that would get the news to his ears faster.

Detective Simmons listened to the caller for a moment, then simply said, "Where?"

The way she said it told everyone in earshot the news wasn't good. Josh fought to breathe in the oppressive July humidity. If they said Andrea was dead, he'd dedicate the rest of his life to wiping the guys who did it off the face of the planet.

Simmons cut the call and stood tapping her finger on the screen, seeming to formulate the words in her head. She stared across the asphalt at the building and didn't address anyone directly. "They found the ambulance on Weaver Road. Looks like the same sniper who hit Cameron hit the ambulance driver."

One of the officers hardened his gaze. "They're tying up loose ends."

Simmons nodded. "If they're taking care of their own, then they must think they have what they need. We know they're headed to the self-storage place over on Whitesville. We need more guys out there, but tell them to stay back unless absolutely necessary." She turned to a plainclothes officer on her right. "We'll have to be careful, because that place is wide open and easy to watch."

Josh moved to step with them, but Simmons pinned him into place with a hard gaze.

She spoke before he could. "Go home. These guys have already proven they'll kill anyone, whether they're a threat or not. We've got to worry about Ms. Donovan. There's no reason to worry about you, too."

They were gone before Josh could argue, but anger still blew through him like the tornado that had struck post a while back. He'd been to combat more times than he cared to count, was probably more highly trained than any three of them combined and they seated him on the sidelines like an injured rookie. He planted the side of his fist in the hood of his rental car, leaving a dent in the dull beige metal. His fist stung and his elbow yowled, but the blow to his masculinity was more than enough to cripple him.

Josh tugged on the hem of his T-shirt and paced to the other side of the parking lot.

A young officer standing nearby glanced at him and smiled sympathetically. "Dude, you're wearing me down."

Josh flashed him a bitter look and kept pacing.

"Man, I know being benched is no fun, but wearing a hole in the asphalt isn't going to bring her back any faster."

Josh shook his head and stalked back to his rental car, where he wouldn't have to look at the officer's sympathetic gaze. This kid didn't know a thing about what *being benched* was like. He was probably barely out of the academy, and here he was trying to feed Josh platitudes. "Don't need a bodyguard. Or a babysitter."

"You sure about that?" Josh opened his mouth to speak, but the officer held up his hand. "I know you're a smart guy. My guess is, at your rank and with your combat tours behind you, you wouldn't still be breathing if that wasn't the case. But men do crazy things when the woman they love is in danger. Somebody keeping an eye on you might be smart."

Josh sank against the front of the car. The woman he loved. He was late to the ballgame. Last night, as they talked, he should have told her. Now it was possible he'd lost the chance forever.

The officer's radio crackled and he listened, then stepped away from Josh to speak, preventing him from making any more comments that would fuel Josh's ire. If he said another word, Josh was liable to haul him to the counseling center and stuff him into that ceiling that Cameron was so fond of hiding in.

The counseling center. Something dug in his mind, something that happened there that didn't fit. He played back their morning visit in his mind, each word, each face, each event.

It's a good thing we had eyes on the building, so we were able to move in fast, otherwise, we wouldn't have known there was trouble. Detective Simmons's words melded with an image, one of Mr. Miller shuffling away from the scene, cell phone to his ear...

Not calling the police.

Josh straightened. If Mr. Miller didn't call the police, then who was he so intent on reaching at that moment? When they were out in the open and vulnerable?

It was the slimmest of threads, thinner than a spider's web, but like that web, he couldn't shake it. If Miller was involved, was working against Andrea, would he risk taking her anywhere near his business? Would he take her back to the place where this all started?

To his knowledge, not a soul was at the counseling center. If the people behind this truly were afraid that Andrea knew something, they'd still go after Cameron's file and anything else that might be at the center. It was a slim chance but it was better than no chance at all.

Josh yanked the keys from his pocket. Before Andrea vanished, Simmons had said they were free to go. Nobody had since told him differently.

He eyed the handful of policemen in the parking lot. If he told them his suspicions, would they sit him on the sidelines again, making him wait until they went to the counseling center to check things out?

That wasn't a risk he was willing to take.

Without a word of explanation, he slipped into his car

and eased out of the parking lot, hoping not to attract any-one's attention. If they wanted to follow him, fine, but he couldn't have them calling a halt. He had to save Andrea, even if that meant following a wild hunch on his own.

SIXTEEN

Andrea ran through her rapidly deteriorating options. From her prison in the backseat of the SUV between two considerable walls of muscle, there was no discernible way out. Aside from the driver, Miller and the two men obviously assigned to her, two more tough guys sat in the third row. Even the president couldn't be this well guarded.

It hit her like a line drive to the forehead. Whoever Mr. Miller really was, whether he was the ringleader of the whole operation or just the head of the hired guns, he was afraid of her and of what she might know. The only thing she couldn't figure out was how to parlay that into more time on the clock of her life.

Mr. Miller's cell trilled, and Andrea jumped so suddenly she cleared the seat.

The man on her right chuckled.

The call ended quickly, with very little said on this end, but Miller clicked it off and pocketed it, the slightest smile on his face.

"They got the stuff?" It was the first time the driver had spoken since they left the church parking lot.

"It was all just sitting there on a pallet in the middle of the storage unit. They're on the move now." Miller shook his head and glanced back at Andrea. "That'll make a nice little nest egg in case we really do have to shut down the operation and move."

Andrea dredged up every ounce of bravado she had left. "Good thing you didn't have to kill them. If you wipe out all of your men, who would be left to protect you?"

"Who says I need protecting?"

"You don't look like the healthiest of men to me. Without your guns here, probably I could take you one on one. Where are you moving if we shut you down here?"

Miller arched an eyebrow and glanced at his counterparts on either side of her. "I could tell you, but then I'd have to kill you." His amusement wasn't lost on her, or on every other man in the car. They all laughed at the joke.

"You're going to kill me, anyway."

"I was genuinely hoping to avoid killing you or your undercover cop friend because murder, especially when it's a cop, makes people take a little too much notice."

"Looks like we're way past that now."

"Surely we're better friends than that. If I really wanted you dead, I would have spiked your coffee weeks ago. Why so cynical?"

She shook her head, shocked she could remain so calm. "Not cynical. Just a realist."

"You watch too many movies." He flicked another loaded look to his companions, then turned to the front as the car veered onto 185.

Miller might not tell her where they were going, but he was already talking too much, and each bit of information he dropped was one more nail in Andrea's coffin. He'd never say names or speak so casually about their plans if he were simply going to drop her by the side of the road and leave town forever.

Andrea held her breath as they blew down the highway, aware that Miller leaned forward, as well, as though he could get them to their destination faster by doing so. She'd welcome the sight of white police cars blocking the lanes more than she'd welcome her next breath.

They were past the airport before Miller relaxed and Andrea felt her last hope deflate. If they hit 280 and headed into the country on the other side of post, there were too many places for her to be lost forever.

"You sure this is where you want to leave her?" The driver's eyes met her impassively in the rearview mirror, as though she were a bag of rotting garbage that needed to be disposed of sooner rather than later.

"Yeah. But first take us back to her office and see what's going on there. If it's still quiet, we may have some work to do."

The SUV swung onto the Victory Drive exit and roared toward the counseling center.

"What work?" Andrea's heart beat faster. Nothing good could come from going back to the center. Nothing.

"We've been through your apartment and didn't find anything, but you have to have notes on us somewhere. You have a fairly secure facility in that office. Any notes you've been keeping on us, seems like they'd be there. And Cameron was fond of leaving clues behind, as well. The way he was writing his own insurance policies, there's a high chance some of them name us. The problem is, we don't have time to search for them." Miller kept his focus on the passenger window, never diverting his attention, even as the vehicle slowed to turn into the counseling center parking lot. "Any thinking man will tell you the best thing is to make sure nothing in there is recognizable, just in case there's any more evidence to point fingers our way. I'm thinking we might need a little bonfire."

* * *

By the time Josh hit the parking lot of the gas station, the sun hung high in the sky, rippling waves off the asphalt. Behind the glass front of the attached convenience store, four people moved among the aisles. A large energy drink poster blocked his view of the cashier, who may or may not have been Mr. Miller himself.

Nothing moved at the counseling center next door. Not even a discarded plastic grocery bag blew across the asphalt.

Any hope he'd had deflated, as if he'd made the third out in the bottom of the ninth. It was his last good swing, and he'd totally missed the ball.

Think, Walker. Think. Where would they take her? They could be anywhere by now, even halfway to the other side of the world. *God, where is she?*

The sound of tires crunching over gravel stopped his self-condemnation. A late-model SUV crept into the counseling center parking lot and disappeared around the back of the building.

Andrea. It had to be the men who had Andrea.

He eased his window down and tuned his ears to the faint sounds coming from the back of the building. One. Two. Three. Four doors slapped shut on the vehicle. With no way to know how many people climbed out those doors or how armed they might be, he didn't dare move to investigate.

This was a familiar sense of helplessness. Once again, here he sat possibly only feet away from a woman in danger, and he was paralyzed by circumstances beyond his control. A dozen tactical scenarios played out, but none of them would help a man with no weapon and no idea who his adversaries were. Josh gripped the steering wheel. If only there was a way to know she was definitely with them, that rushing in and putting his life in danger had a purpose.

As if on cue, a scream cut the air. "Somebody—" The rest of the words were muffled and choked.

His feet hit the pavement before his brain knew he'd moved. Andrea. She was still alive. And only feet away. Close enough to reach yet a million miles distant.

He stopped himself and let his eyes scan the building, trying to formulate a plan. Years of training kicked in, forcing him to seal his emotions into a box and to view the scene with calm pragmatism.

First he had to know what he was up against. That required a recon of the back of that building. As he ran back to the car, new sounds erupted. Doors slammed, tires squealed and the SUV roared around the side of the building, blasting onto Victory Drive toward the highway without stopping for oncoming traffic.

The activity shattered his plans. Was Andrea in that vehicle? He swung his attention back to the counseling center. Or was she inside, possibly…

No. He couldn't believe this was over, that he'd found her only to lose her.

A flicker of movement in the lobby pulled him closer. Somebody was in there. He scanned the parking lot and made a dash for the building.

The sickly sweet aroma of gasoline wrapped around Josh's throat and dragged him back in time, tried to incapacitate him, to remind him of his weakness. Instead of the building, his memory raised a car engulfed in flames. Shaking his head as if to erase the haunting memories of the long-ago nightmare, he focused on the counseling center. Flames rolled out of the storage room off the lobby, licking at the floor, leaving blackened slashes to autograph their territory. The window nearest the fire cracked, a streak running like lightning across the glass before it shattered into jagged pieces.

Nausea roiled his body in racking waves. *God, anything but this. Anything.* He wasn't even sure she was in there. How could he even contemplate diving into that hell?

But somewhere, something deep inside told him he had to. This wasn't about proving himself or atoning for a past that was long forgiven. As well as he knew his own name, he knew Andrea was in that building, and dead or alive, he was the only one in the position to bring her out.

"Hey! You need help?" The shout came from behind him.

Josh whirled to find several people at the gas pumps next door, watching with growing interest. "The building's on fire. Call 911." He ran for the broken window and stepped forward with cautious urgency. Could he do it? With an aching arm to remind him of last time, could he step into that burning building?

"Don't do it!" The voice came again, frantic this time. "Don't try to be a hero, dude!"

Hero. The word tried to trip him up and belittle him. No, he wasn't any more of a hero than the next guy, but he knew what he had to do. It was incongruous, the thoughts in his head in the face of a living nightmare, but it was true. He'd worn failure like a warped badge of dishonor. It was past time to rip that thing off and replace it with the truth.

That was it. If the situation he was in didn't hold so much urgency, he'd stop right now and drop to his knees. All along with Andrea, he'd done exactly what he could do, pushed himself to the limits of his human ability. It was up to God to do the rest.

Just like with Lauren. Just like with Brendan. Saving

them hadn't been up to him. He hadn't been given the gift of knowledge and opportunity.

This time, he had both.

He pulled straighter, standing tall against the weight of gasoline-fueled failure.

Sucking in a breath tinged with the blackened smoke of history, Josh turned his good shoulder toward the smoke roiling out of the window and plunged into the unknown.

Mr. Miller kept a firm grip on Andrea's wrist. She balked at being dragged into her windowless office, away from all hope of being seen. He jerked her arm and she stumbled into the room behind him, crashing into the chair in front of her desk. He shoved her into the seat and looked down, all pretense of kindness evaporated. "What else do you know?"

"I didn't know anything in the first place." She kept her voice defiant. He might kill her, but she'd never let him believe he'd gotten into her head, and he'd sure not destroy her soul. *The Lord is with me; I will not be afraid. What can man do to me?*

"I'm running out of patience." He glanced over his shoulder at the door at the popping sound of the fire, then yanked the gun from his side and held it to her forehead. "Where are your notes? I want everything Cameron told you. Everything you passed on to the detective. Now."

"They're not here." That part was true. Since they didn't exist, the notes sure couldn't be in her office. If she could lead these men on a wild goose chase, maybe it would buy Josh and the police the time they needed to find her.

"Where?"

"I'd have to take you."

"We don't have time for this." Miller shook his head

and yanked the cord from the phone on her desk, his eyes never leaving hers. "You're smarter than I gave you credit for."

For a second, Andrea thought he was going to wind the cord around her neck, but he forced her hand down to the chair and wrapped the thin cable around her wrist.

Andrea kicked and fought, trying to land a knee or a foot anywhere she could, but Miller braced his shin across her thigh and worked faster. "I was going to shoot you, but you know what? I can't. It must be that I'm getting soft, but I got too attached over coffee to look you in the eye while the life bleeds out of you." A thin sheen of sweat broke out on his forehead as Andrea continued to fight. "Still, as much as you'd like me to, I'm not taking you out of here with me."

Andrea yanked her wrist, but the cable only pulled tighter, cutting into her flesh. "And you're not going to let me walk out of here alive, either."

"Good guess." He threaded the cord around itself and tested the tightness. "You're right."

As he said the words, something in the lobby exploded, and the smell of gasoline assaulted her nose. "You're going to burn this place down. With me in it." She couldn't stop the panic from cutting into her voice this time, her nerves as tightly wound as the binding around her wrist. The trembling set in, knocking her knees together. "I'd be better off if you shot me."

"Probably. But you can't always get what you want, and I have to get back to my gas station next door so I can call the fire department and report this tragedy."

The brutality of the man in front of her stunned Andrea as all options dwindled. This was it. No one was coming. If she had realized this morning that this would be her last day, she wouldn't have censored herself in front of Josh, would have told him she loved him, even if the feeling was only in the immature, first-blush stages. He'd have at least had that after she was gone.

A figure materialized in the increasing red glow of the doorway. Josh. Shoulders squared, fists clenched, he stared hard into her eyes, then deliberately slipped his gaze to the gun in Miller's hand.

Andrea drew in a deep breath and lashed out with a foot that caught her captor square in the kneecap. The gun clattered to the floor as he staggered back.

With a roar that tore the air, he shed the facade he'd worn since the first moment he met her and drew back his fist.

The impact hardly registered as Andrea slammed head-on into overwhelming darkness.

The white-hot anger that hit Josh's veins rivaled the heat building behind him.

As Andrea slumped forward and Miller pulled his fist back to strike again, Josh dipped low and charged, his shoulder catching the older man in the back.

They hit the floor with a crash, the bulk of Miller's body landing hard at an angle that forced Josh sideways against the chair holding Andrea prisoner.

The impact rattled Josh's sinuses and whipped his head backward into the desk, blowing dark spots across his vision. While he tried to pull his world back into focus, Miller rolled away.

He moved with surprising agility for a man of his size as he scrambled for the gun. He was nearly on his feet when Josh shook the last of the stars clear and lunged low, striking Miller in the hip and driving him into the ground.

Above the older man's labored breathing, the crackling flames filtered into the room, pulsing a new urgency through Josh's consciousness. If the fire reached that door, they were done. No window. No way out. As soon as this was all over, he was ripping a hole through that wall himself.

"Where did you come from?" Miller choked out the words as he struggled to gain traction on the low pile of the carpet.

Josh drew in a deep breath. He wanted to respond, but the burn of fire and smoke was growing hotter by the second. He glanced at the door. It was still clear, though smoke filtered in along the ceiling. Dialoguing was out of the question.

In that instant of distraction, Miller rolled, throwing Josh off balance. Before he could recover, the other man pulled back his fist and drove it into the telltale scar by Josh's elbow.

The impact tore a guttural yell that was equal parts pain and anger from his throat. White-hot agony shot into every nerve ending. He rolled to his side, fighting for strength, resisting the desire to curl into a ball and cradle his injured arm.

The advantage was enough. Without waiting to see if Josh would return the blow, Miller bolted around the desk, grabbed the gun and aimed it straight at Josh. "You should have counted on me knowing your weakness. I do my homework."

Every ounce of fight seeped out of Josh. Yes, he did have a weakness. It had cost one person her life already, and now it would take everything. The past flooded his judgment. Every time he blinked, he saw his SUV burning, felt the overwhelming helplessness of a body rebelling. *God, help me.* Otherwise he'd fail again, and this time Andrea would pay the price.

From the chair, Andrea groaned, her head rolling slightly to one side. She was coming around.

That was all Josh needed. He drew on what he'd told himself outside. Hope. There was still hope. Josh rose to his knees, arm cradled against his stomach.

Something that looked like concern flickered across Miller's face as the air in the room grew thicker. He glanced at the door, then stepped around the desk to stand directly behind Andrea. His eyes held Josh's as he brushed the hair away from her face and shook his head in mock sadness. "Shame, isn't it? One more you couldn't save. I should shoot her and let you live with that. It would be poetic."

Fury drove Josh to his feet. She wouldn't die because of him. Before he could tempt Miller's trigger finger, Andrea threw her head back. The momentum launched the chair backward, catching Miller at the waist. His eyes widened as he stumbled, lost his footing and crashed into the corner of the filing cabinet. He sprawled into a motionless heap as Andrea landed hard on her back on the floor.

Josh rushed for her, looking down at green eyes that fluttered against unconsciousness.

"See? I knew you could do it." Her eyes slipped shut again.

No. He let his head drop against her forehead. "Come on, Andrea." His whisper was nearly drowned out by the increasing roar from the lobby. It was getting harder to breathe as the fire sought oxygen. Sweat beaded along his back. He reached for her. Pain razored up his right arm, sapping his breath. There was no way. No way he could carry her out.

Miller groaned, and Josh was instantly alert, pivoting to take on a renewed attack. But the man was motionless. Blood streamed from a cut at Miller's temple, and the man was clearly unconscious, though Josh could see him breathing.

Assured that there was no immediate threat, he turned his attention back to Andrea. His eyes burned. He had to find a way to get her out, injured arm or not. Then he'd decide what to do about Miller. He wouldn't fail this time. He couldn't. This was Andrea. And he was not going to lose her.

First things first. Josh clawed at the knots in the phone cord with his left hand, thanking God that the material prevented Miller from pulling the wired plastic into tighter knots. His jaw refused to loosen and sent throbbing pain through his cheek as the room heated and the smoke grew darker. Breathing was harder by the moment. The rank smell of burning synthetics made him gag.

The lights flickered once and vanished, leaving the room shrouded in a gray darkness, lit only by the light of the front lobby filtering in through the smoke-filled doorway. Everything in him screamed for faster movement, but he kept his pace slow and methodical until all of the knots were pulled free. He coughed. The air wasn't just smoky, it was scalding.

His body ached, muscles competing with his arm for attention. The rapidly thinning oxygen and adrenaline pounded his pulse in his ears. His mind ran a continuous loop. *You cannot fail. You cannot fail.* It drowned out every other voice, including the one that told him he should give up because success was impossible.

The last knot worked free, allowing Andrea to slump lower against the floor. When Josh had learned how to carry injured soldiers off the field in combat, he'd never dreamed it would one day be the woman he was falling in love with that he'd have to haul out of danger. With his strength ebbing quickly, he rolled her onto her side and eased her into a sitting position. He slipped his left shoulder against her stomach and draped her upper body across his back, allowing her weight to pull him as he stood on legs that quaked from the stress of the moment.

The air was thinner up here, clogged with smoke, but he couldn't crawl and still carry Andrea out of the building. Ducking as low as he dared, Josh said a final prayer, pulled in as deep a breath as he could and plunged through the door into the lobby, clinging to Andrea by sheer willpower.

The light was an eerie mix of red fire and white daylight, darkening with more smoke by the second. Flames engulfed the wall on the far side of the room and crept behind the receptionist's desk. Heat clawed at his skin. All of his worst nightmares breathed in front of him, worse than he'd ever imagined.

When he burst through the front of the counseling center, his pulse throbbed in black light behind his eyes. The air he drew in had never been sweeter.

People rushed to meet them, pulling Andrea from his arms and laying her gently on the grass median between the counseling center and the gas station. But Josh wouldn't let go.

He knelt beside her and sucked in deep breaths so fast the world started to spin. Bending at the waist, he planted his good hand against his knee and forced himself to breathe normally before he took himself out hyperventilating.

"You okay?" One of the men he'd seen pumping gas earlier leaned low, appearing in his line of sight.

Josh nodded, realizing for the first time that the smell of smoke on him was overwhelming. His arms burned, skin red from the heat. "I'm okay." His voice croaked, burning with a coating of smoke and adrenaline.

In the distance, sirens wailed, but the lobby was rapidly filling with flames. They'd never get here in time to get Miller out of there.

Josh cast a long glance at Andrea, then straightened and stared at the building. He couldn't live with himself if he let that man die. He grabbed the man next to him by the arm. "Don't let her out of your sight." With one final look back, he set off at a run for the door.

"You can't go back in there!" the man yelled after him, but Josh ignored the words and dove through the flames.

The world came back to Andrea with the smell of smoke and pain beyond anything she'd ever felt. The last scene burned into her memory was an expression of murderous hate aimed straight at her.

She awoke screaming against the pain in her jaw and the ache in her lungs.

Gentle hands pressed her down against something soft. "It's okay. The ambulance is here. You'll be fine."

She shook her head. No more ambulances. No. The ambulance would take her away. They'd kill her. The words wouldn't come out past the confusion and the pain locking her jaw tight. A moan split the air around her.

"It's okay. It's a real paramedic this time. I promise."

The voice tugged at her fogged mind, familiar and soothing. Her eyes burned and watered, but she recognized Dutch's face above hers. She worked her jaw back and forth. "Where am I? What's happening?" The questions sapped her strength, rasping out of a throat that felt like a bonfire burned deep inside. Bonfire. Inside. Josh. He'd been in the building. Where was he?

"You're safe, in the parking lot. As for what's happening, you wouldn't believe me if I told you."

She wanted to sit up, call out that Josh was in there,

but darkness clawed and pulled her back, paralyzing her. An EMT slipped an oxygen mask over her face, and the cool rush felt like heaven.

"You inhaled a lot of smoke and you might have a scorch mark or two, but you'll be feeling a whole lot better in no time." Dutch gestured toward her arm. "It's probably not going to feel good for a while, but you're alive. By all indications, you shouldn't be, but you are. Ms. Donovan, it's pretty clear somebody's looking out for you guys."

You guys. "Josh got out?" Her voice muffled against the mask. He had to get out. She needed him. And no one else could die protecting her.

"Josh pulled you out of there." Dutch stared across the parking lot toward the counseling center. He seemed to feel her gaze and looked back down at her. "He's a better man than I am."

Andrea's brows knit in confusion. "Why?"

"He brought you out, then went back in after Mr. Miller. As soon as the paramedics finish with him, my guys will take him into custody. Josh clocked that man good after he hit you."

"But Josh is okay?"

Dutch shifted, and Josh's face appeared in her rapidly clearing vision, sending a jolt through her that had nothing to do with the saline and whatever else was seeping through her veins. "I'm better off than you are."

Andrea lifted her hand and pulled the mask from her face. The tears that spilled from her eyes had nothing to do with the residual burn of smoke. "I knew you'd find me."

He smiled and lifted her hand, pressing a kiss to her palm. "Up until that last second, you were the only one with that much certainty."

"Never doubted it." The words drooped on exhaustion so deep her bones felt unhinged. "How did you get me out?"

Josh gentled the oxygen mask back onto her face. The tang of singed clothes grew stronger as Josh leaned down and pressed a kiss to her forehead, then pulled back. Soot and smoke streaked his face, making his eyes shine brighter. "I raced the fire. They set your storage room on fire first, probably to burn whatever records you have in there and to give Miller time to get out." Smoothing her hair from her forehead, he shifted subjects. "But the better news is they caught your fake detective and his whole crew. They let the guys take the drugs out of the storage unit, then followed them to a rendezvous point. They spilled everything, including where Miller planned to hole up." Josh smiled. "It's over. For real this time."

Relief did more to cool her burning lungs than anything the paramedics had done. "Over?"

"Over." Josh grinned wider and laid a kiss at her hairline. "Except for us. We're just getting started."

EPILOGUE

"You have a warped sense of humor bringing me here." Andrea laughed as she slid from Josh's truck and slammed the door behind her, arching her back to relieve the stiffness from the drive. She caught the baseball glove he threw over the hood and held it against her chest, surveying the ball field.

The trees on the fringes glowed red and gold in the midday sun. The grass of the outfield expended the last of its green for the year, giving way to autumn's advance. Crisp air soothed her lungs, which were still grateful for every pain-free breath she drew. Andrea had spent months in therapy sessions, finally letting go of her brother, starting on a new path in her own counseling, where she could aid in healing without feeling like she bore her patients' burdens on her own shoulders.

The freedom was amazing.

Josh stood shoulder to shoulder with her, drawing on his own glove. "A warped sense of humor? Thanks. Thanks a lot, Donovan." Reaching into the back of the truck, he pulled out a baseball from a bag and flipped it to her, then stood and surveyed the field. "Lots of memories here." He tipped his head toward home plate. "Especially of what the view of those bleachers over there used to look like from third base."

"Really?" Andrea slapped him in the chest with her glove. "Don't be cocky."

"Was I being cocky?" He grinned and winked, then walked backward toward the infield, holding his glove up for her to toss the ball to him.

"You sure about this?" Digging the ball into the palm of her glove, Andrea studied Josh. Against his wishes, he'd gone into physical therapy for the stress on his arm. Now he claimed he was "all better" and ready to come off physical restrictions and back onto full duty at work.

He motioned toward himself with the glove, then held it out again. "It's all good. Promise. It's not like I'm going to be firing the thing from third to home during the World Series or anything." His grin spread wickedly. "I mean, I'm just playing catch with a girl, right? How hard can that be?"

Andrea's spine stiffened. "Yeah? It's on now. You never should have said that." She fired the ball with all of the power she possessed.

Josh caught it neatly and studied it. "That all you got?"

"Get over yourself."

"How can I when you keep looking at me like you adore me?" He held up his free hand to stop her words and jerked his head toward first base. "Enough. Come closer so I don't have to throw so far."

Letting the jokes drop, she jogged over and caught his throw, then took in her surroundings. It had been half a lifetime since she'd been on this field, catching baseballs when Brendan insisted on practicing over the summer. She could almost hear him laughing at her awkward pitches, then his grudging admiration as she improved right along with him. For the first time since he died, the good memories overran the bad and allowed her to smile.

Without thinking, she swung her gaze to third base, the image of high school Josh replaced by the image of him as she knew him now, tall and strong, her fierce protector, a man who leaned on God in a way that almost made her envious. Who'd have thought all those years ago it would come to this?

"Hey, get your head in the game." Josh heckled her from his spot near the pitcher's mound. "What's got you so distracted?"

"Me. Brendan." She lobbed an underhanded toss to him, her tennis shoe squeaking on the grass. "Us."

The ball thwacked against the leather of his glove, but he didn't look at it. Instead, he kept his focus on her. "You know, back in high school I only *thought* I loved you."

She smiled as he fidgeted with the ball in the pocket of his glove. "Is that so?"

"Now I know for sure."

It wasn't the first time either of them had said the words, but the nostalgia of the setting, the perfect temperature of the breeze and the bright sun on fall leaves made them seem weightier than they ever had before. So did the look on Josh's face. Andrea toed the grass and swallowed the emotion that threatened to overwhelm her. "Love you, too." She straightened her stance. "Now throw the ball."

Josh wound up like he was about to throw a Major League pitch, then shifted and arced the ball in an underhanded lob. It hit her glove with a dull thud unlike any catch she'd heard before. Sure enough, when she spread her fingers, a heavy white box rested against the leather.

The sight sent a shock through her that skipped her heart then restarted it in double time. She didn't dare hope he was about to…

He was.

Surprise and joy mingled into one emotion as she turned her focus from the box to the man in front of her, now on one knee. “So will you?”

Andrea dropped to his level, her knees driving hard into the ground, and wrapped her arms around his neck. “Do you have to ask?”

Her kiss was all the answer he needed, melding together their past dreams and their shared future in a present Andrea hoped to hold for the rest of her life.

* * * * *

Dear Reader,

I hope you enjoyed your time with Andrea and Josh in Columbus, Georgia! We had the privilege of being stationed there twice, and it holds a special place in our lives because our daughter was born at Fort Benning.

This book was born when my husband was on his last deployment in Afghanistan. I looked at the calendar and at the thirty-something days stretching out ahead of me until he came back and decided there had to be something to focus on other than the day he'd be wheels down on Tennessee soil again. So I challenged myself to write a book before he came home. Oh, it was exhausting and it needed a whole lot of editing after "The End" was typed, but I fell in love with the story.

When Andrea and Josh started "talking" to me, their voices came wrapped in a whole lot of misconceptions and lies that they believed. They weren't good enough. They were failures. They could never redeem themselves from past mistakes both real and imagined. These two characters tapped into some of the deepest parts of me. After all, we all fear rejection. We all have those things we've done that we wonder if even God is big enough to forgive and heal.

As someone who refers to the lowest point in her life as "the big ugly," I'm here to tell you… God can forgive absolutely anything. Not only that, if you give it to Him, He will somehow manage to make it beautiful and hand it back to you in a way you never saw coming, in a way that He can use for His glory. Believe me, like Ephesians 3:20 says, He really can "do immeasurably more than all we ask or imagine, according to his power that is at work within us" (NIV). You think that thing you did or are doing is beyond His redemptive power? Go to Him. Give it to Him. Then watch what He does. Trust me. I've been there. And more than once, I've shed tears over what He has done, what I never would have dared to have the audacity to dream.

Thank you for reading *Crossfire.* I pray you see God in it and meet Him in a whole new way!

Jodie Bailey

Questions for Discussion

1. The guiding verse for *Crossfire* is Psalm 147:3: "He is the healer of the brokenhearted. He is the one who bandages their wounds." Have you ever experienced God's healing of a broken heart in your life? How?

2. Andrea believes that by helping others she is making atonement for not recognizing her brother's needs. Have you ever tried to earn redemption rather than going to God and accepting His forgiveness?

3. Many of Andrea's actions as a counselor are driven by guilt. When is a time in your life when you acted out of guilt? What happened as a result?

4. Despite Josh's successes in life, he can only see his failures. Why is it so easy for us to see where we've failed and so hard for us to see where we've succeeded?

5. How do you "reset" your perspective and see your successes in light of God's work in your life?

6. It can be hard to sit still and wait. Andrea and Josh made the mistake of moving forward when they should have let the police handle the situation, and it led to more trouble. Why is it so hard to wait? Have you ever moved forward with something when you should have had patience? What happened?

7. Discuss a time in your life when you, like Josh, tried to be the "hero" instead of allowing God to guide your actions.

8. Throughout the novel, Josh and Andrea assume they know what one another is thinking. It often prevents them from communicating openly and honestly. How are assumptions and lack of communication detrimental to a relationship? What can you do to strengthen communication in your own relationships?

9. When Andrea learns who Dutch and Mr. Miller are, she feels betrayed by two men whom she trusted. Has someone close to you ever betrayed you? How did you respond? How did you learn to trust again?

10. In order to rescue Andrea, Josh has to face his worst fears and his own limitations. When was a time in your life when you had to confront the thing that scared you the most? What happened? How did it change you?

11. Did you guess who the villain was? How?

12. Did the setting near a military base intrigue you? Why or why not?

13. What is your favorite type of hero and why?

14. Andrea has a tough job as a counselor. Have you had to counsel someone who was facing a rough time? How did you approach the situation?

15. Who was your favorite character in the book and why?

COMING NEXT MONTH FROM
Love Inspired® Suspense

Available February 4, 2014

THE BABY RESCUE
Witness Protection
Margaret Daley

U.S. marshal Colton Phillips and FBI agent Lisette Sutton have joined forces to blow open a child smuggling ring. But when a stakeout goes horribly wrong, can they track down the kidnapper before a child disappears forever?

TREACHEROUS SLOPES
Terri Reed

Targeted by a stalker, world-class ski jumper Nick Walsh teams up with reporter Julie Frost to find the culprit. Soon they discover some people will do anything for the gold—even murder.

ROYAL WEDDING THREAT
Protecting the Crown
Rachelle McCalla

After attacks endanger the royal nuptials, wedding planner Ava Wright must depend on Royal Guard Jason Selini to protect her. But past secrets may keep Ava from ever having a future....

MOTIVE FOR MURDER
Carol J. Post

The death of her estranged sister has left Jessica Parker with dozens of questions. Undercover FBI agent Shane Dalton may have answers, but can they uncover the truth before a killer strikes again?

LOOK FOR THESE AND OTHER LOVE INSPIRED BOOKS WHEREVER BOOKS ARE SOLD, INCLUDING MOST BOOKSTORES, SUPERMARKETS, DISCOUNT STORES AND DRUGSTORES.

LISCNM0114

REQUEST YOUR FREE BOOKS!

2 FREE RIVETING INSPIRATIONAL NOVELS PLUS 2 FREE MYSTERY GIFTS

YES! Please send me 2 FREE Love Inspired® Suspense novels and my 2 FREE mystery gifts (gifts are worth about $10). After receiving them, if I don't wish to receive any more books, I can return the shipping statement marked "cancel." If I don't cancel, I will receive 4 brand-new novels every month and be billed just $4.74 per book in the U.S. or $5.24 per book in Canada. That's a savings of at least 21% off the cover price. It's quite a bargain! Shipping and handling is just 50¢ per book in the U.S. and 75¢ per book in Canada.* I understand that accepting the 2 free books and gifts places me under no obligation to buy anything. I can always return a shipment and cancel at any time. Even if I never buy another book, the two free books and gifts are mine to keep forever.

123/323 IDN F5AC

Name (PLEASE PRINT)

Address Apt. #

City State/Prov. Zip/Postal Code

Signature (if under 18, a parent or guardian must sign)

Mail to the **Harlequin® Reader Service:**
IN U.S.A.: P.O. Box 1867, Buffalo, NY 14240-1867
IN CANADA: P.O. Box 609, Fort Erie, Ontario L2A 5X3

Are you a current subscriber to Love Inspired Suspense books and want to receive the larger-print edition? Call 1-800-873-8635 or visit www.ReaderService.com.

* Terms and prices subject to change without notice. Prices do not include applicable taxes. Sales tax applicable in N.Y. Canadian residents will be charged applicable taxes. Offer not valid in Quebec. This offer is limited to one order per household. Not valid for current subscribers to Love Inspired Suspense books. All orders subject to credit approval. Credit or debit balances in a customer's account(s) may be offset by any other outstanding balance owed by or to the customer. Please allow 4 to 6 weeks for delivery. Offer available while quantities last.

Your Privacy—The Harlequin® Reader Service is committed to protecting your privacy. Our Privacy Policy is available online at www.ReaderService.com or upon request from the Harlequin Reader Service.
We make a portion of our mailing list available to reputable third parties that offer products we believe may interest you. If you prefer that we not exchange your name with third parties, or if you wish to clarify or modify your communication preferences, please visit us at www.ReaderService.com/consumerschoice or write to us at Harlequin Reader Service Preference Service, P.O. Box 9062, Buffalo, NY 14269. Include your complete name and address.

LIS13R

SPECIAL EXCERPT FROM

A U.S. marshal must work with an FBI agent to save a child's life. Read on for a preview of the next exciting book in the WITNESS PROTECTION *series, THE BABY RESCUE by Margaret Daley, available February 2014*

FBI agent Lisette Sutton entered supervisory U.S. marshal Tyler Benson's office in Denver, and two men rose. In front of the oak desk, the larger one of the pair was probably Deputy Marshal Colton Phillips, the person she would be teamed with in this case involving child smuggling and baby brokering across state lines.

As she took a seat, she slid a glance toward U.S. marshal Phillips. He swung his gaze toward her. His startlingly blue eyes fringed in long lashes caught hold of her, and for a moment she couldn't look away. Intense. Focused. Assessing, as she had. Her stomach fluttered. Slowly one corner of his mouth tilted up, and he glanced away—turning his attention to his supervisor, who was talking.

"From what Don Saunders has given us so far, we're dealing with a black market baby adoption ring that covers a good part of the United States," Benson said.

Benson cleared his throat. "Now that Saunders is here in Denver and settled into a safe house, we need more. He has additional information he'd promised the marshals in St. Louis once he was out of the area. Time to question the man, and if he's bluffing, call him on it if he wants to remain in WitSec."

"From my boss I heard there was an incident yesterday in St. Louis. What happened?"

"A couple of guys interrupted our transport to the airport," Colton said. "I talked with Marshal McCall in St. Louis this morning. They have interrogated the three men involved in the wreck and run background checks. There doesn't appear to be any connection to the criminal elements in St. Louis."

"Could Don Saunders have orchestrated an escape somehow?"

"Not likely. It's not like he had access to a phone at the safe house, or that he left the place."

"But if he has been compromised in any way, our chance to find out more about this organization and catch others involved will vanish. A smuggling ring like this can't exist. Children are involved."

Phillips sat forward, closer to her. "I know exactly what's at stake with this case."

To find out if Colton and Lisette can work through their differences and solve their case, pick up THE BABY RESCUE, available February 2014 wherever Love Inspired® Suspense books are sold.

Copyright © 2013 by Harlequin Books S.A.

LISEXP0114